Advance Praise for *Maximus in Catland*

"*Maximus in Catland* is a charming book. For those among us who adore felines, as the author clearly does, there is the additional benefit of seeing an alternate history for beloved pets! David Garrett Izzo has written a fable set in a time when big cats were a sentient and, indeed, heroic race, while human beings were the greedy, cruel newcomers. The spiritually aware cats have to counter the power-mad and evil human Reltih, and the trio we first met as kittens—Huxley, Maximus and Princess—now grown, join forces to lead the battle against the human. *Maximus in Catland* has all the necessary ingredients for a successful fairy tale: good and evil, unrequited love and loving loyalty, heroism and ancient wisdom. When one spells the name of the cruel and avaricious human leader backwards, the fable becomes parable, and, much like C.S. Lewis's Narnia books, can be interpreted as straightforward fantasy or something a little deeper."

—Jenny Ivor, *Rambles*

Advance Praise for *Maximus in Catland*

" . . . a world of myth and metaphorical meaning.

"Maximus the First is a giant lion-sized black cat with a shiny white chest and burning yellow eyes. Maximus was stolen as a kitten and cared for in captivity by a wise, magical eagle named Wystan and watched over by a wizard named Gerald. The first half of the book involves Maximus's rescue by the red-and-tan tabby named Huxley.

"The second half recounts Maximus's conflict with the evil humans, likened to Nazis with names that are cyphers for Hitler and Mengele, men who have chosen 'Second Nature' (the Dark side), that is, ego and power over collective identity and common good.

"*Maximus in Catland* is, in fairy-tale style, another examination of the idea of the Truly Strong Man—or, in this case, Cat—which is one who would give his own life for the sake of transpersonal good (what in Catland is called 'Great Mystery').

"I liked this little book. As a cat-lover myself, I thoroughly enjoyed the images of giant housecats bounding to the rescue. Izzo's writing is very descriptive. This book is a treat—with a truly mystical message."

—Toby Johnson, author of *Secret Matter*

Advance Praise for *Maximus in Catland*

"*Maximus in Catland* is an interesting story that grabs the reader and doesn't let them go until the end. The story is a lot of fun. David Garrett Izzo spins a tale of giant cats that ruled the world with mysticism, honor and courage. I found these cats to be everything I wished humans could be today. What a wonderful world it would be if these giant cats really did exist. Overall, I would have to say that this is a very good story and can be read by young adults and adults both. So, if you love cats, whether they are small house cats or large, intelligent, gentle cats, this is the book for you."

—Conan Tigard of *The Reading Nook–Fantasy Place*

Other Works by David Garrett Izzo

A Change of Heart (novel)

Catland (novella)

The American World of Stephen Vincent Benet (play)

Wrath (play)

Christopher Isherwood: His Era, His Gang, and the Legacy of the Truly Strong Man

The Writings of Richard Stern

Christopher Isherwood Encyclopedia

W. H. Auden Encyclopedia

Stephen Vincent Benet (essays)

Thornton Wilder (essays)

Advocates & Activities Between the Wars (essays)

W. H. Auden: Legacy

Aldous Huxley & W. H. Auden on Language

Henry James Against the Aesthetic Movement (essays)

Aldous Huxley's Brave New World*: 75th Anniversary Essays* (forthcoming)

Maximus in Catland

and

Purring Heights

Two Novellas

by

David Garrett Izzo

Arlington, Virginia

Published by Gival Press, an imprint of Gival Press, LLC.

For information please write:

Gival Press, LLC, P. O. Box 3812, Arlington, VA 22203.

Website: *www.givalpress.com*

Email: *givalpress@yahoo.com*

First edition ISBN: 1-928589-34-0 (ISBN 13: 978-1-928589-34-1)

Library of Congress Control Number: 2006924426

Book cover photo "Le Chat Lion" by Casimir.

Format and design by Ken Schellenberg.

Dedication:

To Carol Ann Corrody, her mom Lo, Dude, Mark and Lu, Uncle Martin and Uncle Harold, Dan and Michelle, Billy, Lori, and Maryann, David Powell, my wonderful friend from childhood whom I have remembered for 48 years, and to our cats Huxley, Max, Princess, and Phoebe.

Maximus in Catland

Part One:

Know all that enter here at the Great River that this is a place of peace. Leave your weapons at the river's edge and when you cross the bridge to the other side, you will believe that you are in Catland.

In a time before time was recorded by man, between the dinosaurs and the dawn of written history, there were other worlds before this world as we know it. What was once can be again. But for now one listens in a dream and sees and hears places and sounds that transform what we know into what we want to believe. Before history recorded the ancient Egypt that worshiped cat Gods and built sphinxes to honor them, there was a species of cats that were as large as lions but their faces were like cats as we know them today. Our cats are not descended from lions; rather, lions are descended from those great cats of long ago who could run like the wind on all fours or stand as men do now. In the mysterious yellow, green, and sometimes blue eyes that one sees in cats today, one looked into those ancient cat eyes and saw a touch of some heaven that the great cats sought to find on earth.

And this was Catland.

In Catland, there was a Council of Cats that gave value to love, and to finding the wisdom to love wisely and fairly. With great study over eons, the Council of Cats learned how to raise kittens to strengthen their bodies and their minds, and to find the inner eye that even when their outer eyes were closed, could see visions that would lead them to inner places that would guide them in the outer world. Kittens were raised to honor and cherish nature. They learned that each kitten soul existed always, entering a body before birth where this soul would live. Hence the body was the soul's home and as any home should be made strong to protect and develop this most important occupant. Cat words are spoken between cats to serve the world of Catland and then there is the language without words, an intuition of souls that needs no words but learns to share feelings through quiet eyes that tell much more than words can.

And now the boy cat, Maximus the Second, looks at the night sky through his quiet eyes that are very sad. Maximus the Second had come from his Grandfather Huxley's chamber where the revered leader of the Cat Council was soon to let go of his soul, which would return to the Great Mystery until its chosen future time for another earthly visit. Maximus knew Huxley would rejoin his grandmother, Princess Blue who had left her body the year before. The boy cat did not know that there was another in the Great Mystery that Huxley had missed for a long time. The young Max and his father Matthias would miss the body of the wise Huxley but honor his soul always in their memories. Maximus was watching the night sky from the tower Huxley had built forty years before in order to see if an old friend would return. The boy cat was looking for the Blue Light that would take Huxley's spirit upward.

The great Cat Council had seen peace for forty years in Huxley's leadership, which had begun with the end of a long period of hostility. Now, there were new threats, as the barbarians that had been defeated when Huxley was a young leader, were again massing and making fearful noises that were disturbing Catland once more.

The boy Maximus knew little of such outer concerns, but watched a summer storm of thunder and lightning that reminded him of his lessons. He'd learned that his spirit was as powerful as nature itself and he knew that young cats need not be afraid of nature's power but should know that they share in it, and should take strength from it. The boy cat Maximus had learned that when he heard the thunder, not to be afraid of it, as this thunder was the sound behind the sound and that the lightning was the light behind the light that come from the Great Mystery. The sound behind the sound was a living thing that cats knew well for the purr of happiness deep in their bodies was also from the Great Mystery.

With the thunder, nature was announcing that a path was opening and Max believed, as he and all kittens learned, that grandpa Huxley would be making the journey of the blue light back to the Great Mystery from which all cats came. This night the Great Mystery would be even greater.

The thunder came, as it had never been heard before as though to crack the sky wide open. The following lightning was the brightest the boy cat Maximus had ever seen. And in the mini-seconds of their giant flash, Max's inner eye and outer eyes grew wide as caves. For behind the clouds he saw a figure for an instant—a giant cat with a great scarlet cape billowing like a sail while this figure floated like a ghost amidst the heavy rain. The young Maximus was overcome at this strange vision, which repeated with each brilliant bolt. Fearing some disturbance in the opening of the path, he ran to his grandfather's side, calling his name: "Grandpa Huxley! Grandpa Huxley!" Hearing his son's voice, his father, Matthias, also made haste to Huxley's chamber.

The old cat was awake and smiling the sweetest smile when they reached him.

Huxley was still conscious and both he and Matthias heard Maximus describe the vision in the clouds. Grandpa Huxley's smile grew wider and his paw rubbed under Max's chin to calm the boy cat. The old eyes looked into the young eyes and saw the boy Max as well as the boy Huxley had been long before. He asked his grandson: "And this enormous cat whom you say was black with a shining white chest, and a black and white face and giant burning yellow eyes, did he wear a red cape?"

"Yes, grandfather. How did you know?"

The wise old whiskers sighed with grateful recognition. "My precious boy that is no demon—far from it. He is your great uncle, Maximus the First, the legend of Catland. He has come, as he promised long ago, to bring me home to the Great Mystery where he and Princess Blue, your grandmother, wait for me."

The boy Max had known of the Legend of Catland as did all kittens. Maximus the First had been the great protector who gave his body to save his father, Matthias, from the barbarians, and thus insured the long peace that followed. Huxley knew it was time for the boy Max to know his past, as it would also become his future. He was destined to lead Catland after his father, Matthias. The inner eye saw this; now the outer eyes must tell it. Huxley looked at his son, Matthias, and they shared their inner understanding.

Huxley said to Max, "Come my precious boy; sit beside me. It is time for the *Tell*."

This for young kittens was the story of Catland. "But Grandpa, I know the *Tell*."

"Yes, you do, young Max—as it is told in school. Yet, your father and I know even more and you are ready." Huxley reached for his thick wire-rimmed spectacles—his vision was never good but his inner eye more than compensated for his outer eyes. He pointed to a great wooden chest, and Matthias fetched the *Book of Books*, the pawwritten journal of the family's history, which was also a chronicle of Catland.

For the second time on this night, the boy's ears and eyes were as wide as caves.

Forty Years Earlier:
• • • • • • • • • • • • • • • • • •

There are caves of light and caves of darkness. In a dark cave far away from Catland were captured slaves of all kinds and from all places. They were what one now calls animals but in the time before time, these animals were as humans are now and humans were not as advanced as these animals. Humans were a later species and did not yet have the long-earned wisdom of the animals. The humans wished to rule by force. In this place are captured animals that would work in mines or farms or would be sold to rich humans as prizes for display in cages. In this dark place were captured cats from the North of what is now called England. They were strong and broad, great workers and hunters—and they had gifts from the Great

Mystery. These cats, often with black backs, white chests and legs, and round faces with black around their large yellow eyes and white triangles over their mouths and nose, could speak without sound from mind to mind even if the spoken language was different than their own. Few of these cats were left in the world.

One of them, a mother cat, was about to give birth. She had been kidnapped in this condition and was taken so her kittens would be born and then be sold, but her soul would not allow this. She willed that her litter would not be born into slavery, and that her soul would leave her body and return to the Great Mystery. Yet, strangely, she did not stop the birth of one male kitten just before her soul's departure. In a cage next to her own was an eagle taken because his piercing eyes were sitting in a red head topped by a redder plume that was unlike any eagle ever seen. He is Wystan the Wise, who had been the magic leader of Eagleland, a land now without direction since Wystan had gone missing two years before. He was their pilot, the guide who was their bridge to the Great Mystery. Without him, Eagleland was a place of sadness.

Just before the mother cat traveled on the blue light to the Great Mystery, her mind visited the mind of Wystan. He stretched his long wing through the narrow bars. The mother cat lifted the kitten by the neck with her teeth and placed him in the cradle of the great wing. Wystan drew the shivering kitten into his cage and next to his warm body where he hid him under his wing. Then the mother cat's spirit left her body. For the next three months, Wystan would hide the kitten and feed him from the meager food he himself received.

Three Months later:

• • • • • • • • • • • • • • • • •

The fortress of the humans was a natural stronghold of a horseshoe-shaped high mountain plateau with the only entry a narrow opening. Watchtowers surrounded the top of the U-shaped cliffs and sentries could see far in the distance—but only during the day. Night was another matter. Fires could only throw the barest light and the flickering flames created shadows that other shadows could hide in. Trevenen, a Catland senator and general of the Catland Freedom Riders, led six of the dark-cloaked shadows. These cat-warriors defended Catland and led rescue missions. This time the search was personal. The mate of Trevenen, Maria, had visited her relatives in the North of England and did not complete her return trip. She was full with kittens and Trevenen had hoped she would have at least one more son to be a brother to their first son Huxley.

The great cats, the size of lions, had long claws that formed natural grapples. Since they are just as accustomed to stand up-right as to run on all fours, they are excellent climbers. The cats, led by Trevenen, were masters of stealth and silence, able to understand each other with glances and body talk. The five-pointed paws dug in to the nearly sheer steep cliff to circumvent the heavily guarded horseshoe opening. On the plateau's height to each side of this entryway were stacks of deadly rocks sitting on scaffolds built from tree trunks. The guards could toss them down singly or trip a scaffold to release a crushing slide of dozens at a time, burying enemies and also blocking the entry from a flow of possible invaders.

The Freedom Riders reached the crest and looked over. There were fires but few sentries, and none were awake. Quietly the cats descended down the inside wall of the precipice. They saw a cave opening in the rock. Slinking like snakes across the ground, the cats wrapped themselves in their dark cloaks and were as dark as the night itself. Unseen, the cats crawled into the cave. They dispatched drowsy guards into a deeper sleep with single swipes of mighty paws that moved as lightning and could fell elephants, let alone these humans. Yet, the paws had not extended their deadly claws. The cats wanted only to render the humans unconscious, not kill them.

As they neared the rear of this cave, the cats could smell non-human creatures and knew these were the caged captives of many species. Trevenen's twitching snout was dismayed, as it did not recognize Maria's scent or that of any other adult cats. He could smell kittens, but not many. His nose and then his eyes also detected bears, swans and other rare and beautiful birds, horses, and a giant eagle with a great red head. There were even other humans who were not guards but also prisoners. Trevenen knew that there were humans who were peaceful teachers and artists who tried to inform their fellows that the path of the dictators was not the way and could only lead to hate and war. But the majority of humans were followers and yearned to be told what to do and believe rather than think for themselves. It is easy to follow and not feel the weight of personal responsibility. The question then becomes, is there wisdom in the leadership or just an instinct for power? So far human nature seemed to choose the lust for power while the great cats had advanced far beyond that foolish goal and chose peace and the way of love.

Yet, the cats had learned that mysticism alone was not enough to assure safety from enemies outside of Catland. The

Freedom Riders were trained warriors who understood that force was always the last resource when peaceful efforts failed. Kidnapping and slave trading were not matters for negotiation.

Trevenen was a heartbroken warrior as Maria was not here, but he was resolved to complete the mission. The big cats freed the small cats and tiny birds, as their cages were easily broken. The larger cages were more difficult to wreck without noise that would bring the enemy in numbers that would not be overcome. Then no one would be freed. The big cats were ready to exit when the eagle sounded a throaty cooing that turned their heads.

The eagle raised a wing. Beneath it, cuddled to his body, was one more kitten, even more fur and bones than the others were. Trevenen reached cautiously and took the black-backed, white-chested kitten. The little one resisted leaving, clinging to his foster father, the great eagle. Wystan the Wise listened to the little mind speak without words to his mind. Wystan told him not to be afraid. The little mind cried and felt rather than said to the eagle: "I will come back for you." Trevenen's great paw took him and the whiskered jaw nodded at the great eagle. Trevenen had never seen such a thing before, an eagle protecting a kitten instead of eating it. Nor had he ever seen a red-headed eagle. In all ways, Wystan was no ordinary eagle. The Freedom Riders left the cave and in the darkness of night they slithered up and over the cliff and returned to Catland. They hoped that they would never have to return for the next time would not be so easy. Destiny does not always cooperate.

Trevenen tied the kitten to his neck in a sack and felt the little one shiver from fear and cold. The warrior cat hid his tears in the darkness. He had not found Maria. He never would. How could he know that her love was no further than the yellow-eyed kitten that cried for his foster father, the mystical eagle? The old warrior and the near future's greatest warrior were partners in sadness. In a second sack, carried by Trevenen's good friend Julian, was a tiny sparrow, another former captive given his freedom by the Riders. He was so long in a cage that his wings could not fly when Julian wished to let him loose. The cats knew he could not survive until he could fly again and would guard him until that day. His name was Stephen. The sparrow's mind could feel the mind of the kitten and without words told the little one not to be afraid, that he was going home. The kitten's mind asked Stephen if he would stay with him. The sparrow said yes. In this case, destiny did cooperate. They would be lifelong friends and the little sparrow would have a heart much braver than his size.

The sun came up as they neared Catland. The kitten and Stephen could feel the sun's warmth—or was it the warmth that came from Catland itself. Probably both.

Catland was in a valley with a slow winding river. On each side of the clear water the land rose, not sharply, but as a line of gradually rising and falling hills where there was much lush greenery for kittens to play and learn in. In the edges of the hills, the cats burrowed their homes into the soft dirt and made beds and other lounges from the thick leaves, vines, and branches. Outside, cats and kittens loved the sun when it was cool and found shade when it was hot. They even waded in the river during the summer and the braver ones swam across. Cats love to sleep and each has a favorite tree or boulder to snuggle against. From Catland the Riders could hear the Horn of Welcome announcing their return.

An appreciative Catland community welcomed the Freedom Riders. The kitten in the sack peaked out and looked over Trevenen's shoulder. He saw this world where everyone was like himself. And they were all purring with contentment that matched their happy faces. The collective purring droned and was such a calm sound. The kitten was less afraid, especially when he saw more kittens like himself. One such kitten, a little older than the kitten in the sack, ran towards Trevenen and threw himself down to be nuzzled and licked by his father. Their noses marked each other as cats do. The kitten was doing a Floppy, the term in Catland for a child who wishes to receive the gift of love and affection. In Catland, a Floppy is never ignored. Kittens are acting intuitively and never do a Floppy except out of love. The kitten in the sack thought of the redheaded eagle that had also never denied him and the little one became sad. He would never forget Wystan the Wise.

Trevenen's son was Huxley. He was named after his grandfather who was a great scientist. Huxley was a reddish-tan and white striped tabby as was his father. His mother was black and white, but the first kitten usually takes after the father, a second after the mother. Huxley did not yet know his mother was missing rather than just visiting in the north. Trevenen dreaded when he would have to tell Huxley. Trevenen could hardly admit it to himself, hoping against hope that she might still be found. This would not be.

He now hoped to distract Huxley with a mission: the care of this poor little orphan on his neck.

Trevenen said, as he untied the sack and placed it carefully at Huxley's paws, "Look here, my son and see what I found." Out crawled this near-starved kitten whose fur was thin and sparse showing the rib bones that had not any fat whatsoever. As weak and skinny as he was, the kitten was already longer than the older Huxley, and his shoulders and hips were broader though there was hardly a muscle to be seen on them.

Huxley put his twitching nose to the ground and approached the poor orphan. Their noses rubbed and the black and white little one reminded Huxley of his mother. Huxley licked the skin and bones and the kitten purred for the first time since leaving the side of Wystan the Wise. "Father," Huxley sighed, "he is so weak, the poor thing." Huxley tried to lift him with his teeth by his neck as his father, and especially his mother, had done when he was very little. The black and white kitten was too heavy, and Trevenen completed the task as he and Huxley brought the kitten into their burrow near a thick grove of tall and wide-trunked trees. When Huxley brought food, the kitten could not eat fast enough and they worried he'd get a stomachache. When he was finally full, the kitten, exhausted, fell asleep. Huxley did a Floppy and pulled the kitten across his body so he could feel warm and loved. The kitten would cling to his new protector all that day and night. As he slept, Huxley asked his Father. "What is his name?"

"I don't know Huxley," and Trevenen then told Huxley the story of the rescue and the great redheaded eagle. Huxley was spellbound for eagles were almost never seen, and were distant creatures that were thought to be deep into the Great Mystery. Huxley asked, "What should we name him?"

Trevenen and Maria had discussed names for the second son and had decided on a name. Trevenen thought this kitten would be as close to a second son as there would ever be. "We will call him Maximus."

A week later:

There's nothing like a lot of food for a growing kitten! Maximus had put on weight and muscle across his broad shoulders and his fur was turning silky smooth instead of straggly and matted. His size for his age brought exclamations from visitors to Trevenen's burrow. He was going to be a very, very large cat. Maximus and Huxley were already best friends.

Huxley was not as robust as Maximus nor even as strong as kittens his own age, which was, in fact, a year older than Maximus who was already nearly twice as long and wide as Huxley.

Max's friend Stephen the Sparrow was never far away. He was now able to fly again and had built himself quite a nice nest on a lower branch of the nearest tree. His mind spoke to Max's mind, even when they were apart. Sometimes, Huxley would see Maximus rapt with concentration. Huxley imagined that Max was having bad memories of his captivity, which put him in a trance, when, in fact, he was speaking with Stephen.

One morning there was a wildly discordant stream of frantic birdcalls and screeches from outside the burrow. Huxley's cat-ears turned to the sound like wildflowers seeking sun.

Max's ears did the same, but simultaneously he ran with great speed toward the tree of Stephen's home. Huxley followed and saw Max reach the tree in an instant, leap up high on the trunk, and dig in his claws with enormous power. He climbed like a streak to Stephen's branch. There he saw that crows, those sneaky loafers, were trying to force the tiny sparrow from his hard-earned nest and take it for themselves. Imagine their surprise at seeing eye to eye into the now fierce yellow eyes of Maximus, so far up this tall tree where other cats dared not reach. The mind of Maximus told the crows to go build their own nest somewhere else, preferably at the other end of the great valley.

Stephen, nearly out of breath, so that his heart and wings beat like frantic drums, said between rapid gulps of air, "About time. . . . How can I keep my word . . . to stay with you . . . if those big bullies chase me away." Stephen tended to be excitable, but he actually had amazing survival skills. Indeed, he had survived the ice age, the dinosaur age, and many ages since! Stephen was no ordinary sparrow, nor is his presence in any time or place a mere coincidence. Why? The answer lies in the Great Mystery, and was not yet, if ever, to be known to earthbound creatures.

Max's mind answered his critic. "Would it have been better if I waited until they ate you." Stephen shuddered at the thought as he sometimes forgot that he was part of the Great Mystery and could not disappear so easily.

On the ground far below, Huxley had no idea what was going on as he had only seen the crows fly off as the sparrow was still cowering in his nest unseen by other than Max.

Huxley called up, "Maximus, are you all right, what happened?"

"Yes, I have saved my friend the sparrow." Then Max looked down to the ground where Huxley seemed a mile away.

Big Mistake!!!!!!!!!!!!!!

Max's eyes became doubled in size as he realized how high he was, and freezing, he dug his claws in deeper. Going up was much easier than going down. His protective instinct got him up the tree, but now he was afraid to return to earth. He could not hang on for much longer. What to do?

Below, Huxley felt something strange in his head. Someone was talking to him without sound, just as his teacher, Gerald would do. It was Stephen telling him to run for his father. "Cling fast, Maximus! I will get help." Huxley returned with Trevenen who looked up in disbelief. No cat Trevenen ever knew could make such a vertical climb with just claws alone. "Good gracious, Maximus, Huxley said you were in a tree, but I hadn't imagined how high; you seemed to have flown up."

Trevenen knew he could not climb up himself, as at his size it is one thing to go up a sloping mountain but another to go straight up a vertical tree trunk. "Huxley," Trevenen called, "fetch me the great rope from the burrow." Huxley returned with a hundred-foot long, one-inch thick cord made from dried vines. The Freedom Riders made a circle of the rope at one end and were skilled at tossing the loop around some object in order to make difficult climbs. On a third try, Trevenen curled the rope around the branch of Stephen's nest and pulled the cord toward the trunk where Max clung perilously as his claws were losing their grip and he was slowly sliding down.

"Maximus, you must reach with one paw to wrap the rope around you." Max knew he could not spare even one paw without falling. Stephen, still unseen in his nest, suddenly emerged, and from below seemed merely a yellow dart. Yet, somehow this yellow speck took the rope in its tiny beak, untied the loop, and tied it again around Max's middle. Huxley and Trevenen could hardly tell the sparrow was a bird and certainly no bird they knew was capable of such a thing—until now. Trevenen gently lowered Max back to the ground. While on his way down, Max thought that, indeed, this rope was a handy thing and he would remember this lesson. The lessons were only beginning. Trevenen asked Max the cause of his adventure. Max explained that his effort was to protect the tiny sparrow that had been rescued by Trevenen first and now Maximus. Trevenen was pleased at this instinct for bravery that matched Max's larger size and muscles for his age.

The Next Morning:

As the sun rose and light entered the burrow, Huxley nuzzled Maximus as cats do to wake him. Both then did those familiar cat stretches, the high arching of the back and then the long, paw-extended stretch forward with their chins nearly touching the fronts of their paws. Then Max lolled on his side and yawned wide trying to shake sleep and embrace consciousness. In mid-yawn, he heard Huxley say, "Gerald said he would come after first light. Father wants you to begin your lessons that I have already begun and I will help you catch up." Maximus knew nothing of school as his life thus far had found him first hidden under an eagle's wing (though at the time he did not realize that the eagle was not his natural father) and next prancing about the splendor of Catland. Could there be a greater contrast? Yet, in thinking of Wystan the Wise, he seemed to recall mind messages that were as if they came to him in sleep. Though he was more than happy to be free, in a different way he missed the safety of that great wing. He would always think of Wystan, as his first father even while Trevenen was quickly becoming his second.

Huxley's back was toward the burrow's opening, while Maximus was opposite him and facing the outside. The early sun cast long shadows and Max, looking over Huxley's shorter shoulder, saw a thin shadow slowly moving closer. "Now, Maximus," Huxley explained, "Gerald does not speak as we do but communicates as you say Stephen the sparrow talks to you. He is very old and knows the ways of the whole world, not just Catland, and . . . " Huxley stopped his talk because he saw Max's face turn into one of great fear and panic. Then Max leaped, reversed himself in mid-air, and headed to the back of the burrow where he proceeded to try and dig his way out, which, of course, would not happen anytime soon as the back of the borrow was the beginning of the rest of the mountain.

From the burrow's entrance, they heard the voice of Gerald's mind, and it seemed so deep and old with a permanent echo that entered into the minds of Huxley and Max.

"Now, Huxley, did you not, as I asked, advise our new friend so as to prepare him for my coming." Huxley did not answer because it was not a matter of forgetfulness, but that he was afraid that if he had told Max, Max might have run away. For you see, Gerald is a human. Gerald understood Huxley's omission and Huxley did a floppy at Gerald's feet. Gerald reached down and vigorously rubbed Huxley's tummy as if an affectionate grandfather. He loved to rub Huxley's beautiful fur, but unlike a cat would, he stopped short of licking him.

He turned his blue eyes to Maximus whose back legs were running in place, and his rear end and tail were sticking out of the newly-made tunnel that he was still hard at digging. Gerald's mind reached into the frightened kitten in a calm yet firm voice. "Maximus, I come in the name of Wystan the Wise who would tell you not to be afraid of his oldest friend."

At the name of the great eagle, the frantic legs stopped churning, and the rear end wiggled in reverse. Maximus turned and faced what he had feared. He saw a tall, very thin human, with a long and lean face, a very straight, narrow nose, above which were the first blue eyes Maximus had ever seen on any living creature. These eyes seemed transparent and Max felt as if he was entering them into a vastness greater than the blue sky over Catland. They were so blue that he imagined that the sky imitated these eyes, which had come first, after which the sky was honored to take their color. Maximus felt what Huxley already knew, that if one could enter those eyes one could know everything.

Still, Maximus was a child—albeit a rather large one—and still quite capable of asking an impertinent question. "Well, then, can you tell me what Wystan looks like?"

Gerald was too kindly to take offense; moreover, he saw that Max was not so ready to believe anything he was told. This was a good thing for a student—or anyone else for that matter. If one does not question, one does not learn; one merely follows. Gerald knew that the greatest fear did not come from tyrants but from the collective ignorance that allowed tyrants to gain power before they could be stopped.

Gerald answered, "Wystan the Wise is an eagle unlike any other for he has a red head topped by a red plume." Gerald saw that Max was pleased, but sensed that Maximus knew someone could have told this to Gerald. "And," Gerald continued, "when your tiny head rested against his body under Wystan's wing, you did not hear a heartbeat as you yourself have, but a continuous drone, almost like purring, that is the sound of the universe."

Maximus was stunned. His response was a floppy for Gerald's soothing hand to rub—but no licking.

The Lesson
• • • • • • • • • •

Maximus asked Gerald how long he had known Wystan. "Hmmmm," and then Gerald scratched at his bearded chin, "It has been so long I cannot recall such a first meeting, or if there ever was one. It just seems we have always known each other in one form or another. . . ." Drifting off, Gerald closed his blue eyes and momentarily he seemed less flesh and bone but timeless, which in fact, he and Wystan are. "I do remember that long ago I was Wystan's teacher as I am yours now; of course, Wystan learned well and now it might be said he is the teacher more so than I."

"Why, then, Gerald," Huxley asked, "is Wystan now captured? How did he let this happen?"

"A good question—if one might think that the body that holds the spirit to be more important than the spirit. On the other paw, who can truly understand the ways of the Great Mystery? I can only assure you that Wystan the Wise is, indeed, *too* wise to be in any particular place, or even in any particular form—this time an eagle—if the Great Mystery did not wish it so. I do know though that the fellow eagles of Eagleland are for the moment a bit lost and Eagleland itself has been shrouded in clouds and the green has gone gray from lack of sun. There is nothing but despair there that will not lift until Wystan returns to them."

Huxley and Maximus were still puzzled. "But Gerald," Huxley continued, "if Wystan has a choice, and his choice affects so many others, why does he not act to free himself?" In Catland, all kittens learned that the needs of the many come before the needs of the few or the one.

"Perhaps, Huxley, Wystan needed to be in the place he is now because he was destined to save Maximus."

With this the silent Maximus resolved then and there that it would be his own destiny to rescue Wystan—even if, as Gerald seemed to indicate, he actually needed rescuing or not. The Great Mystery was great, but there were some decisions that a cat could take into his own paws. Maximus said nothing of this. The time would come when actions would mean more than any words he could say in the present.

For now, Gerald decided to begin the day's lesson but he would not wander too far off from the matters thus far raised.

"Now my clever young kittens, for today's lesson I shall pose a riddle that I learned from Wystan for you to consider—listen closely!

"Private faces in public places are wiser and nicer than
Public faces in private places."

Gerald's riddle initially stimulated nothing but blank stares. Gerald repeated it and followed with the sharp command: "Think of what these words mean alone then put them back together again!"

And with this Huxley put himself in the cat's thinking pose, which is the very pose that the later Egyptians would recreate with their statues of the Sphinx: paws stretched forward and touching together with the head over them deep in thought. Maximus imitated Huxley.

Huxley thought that "public" meant the world of his father as a senator representing the burrows in his district. Trevenen spoke to large assemblies as well as citizens one at a time.

Maximus knew little of "public" as he had lived under an eagle's wing and only rarely could Wystan let him peek his head out although there was little to see in the darkness. Yet, Max did see the shadowed and mute faces of other creatures that were all afraid to make audible sounds. The bears slept for it was winter and did not notice their captivity; the birds were dull, beaks down; sometimes they would frantically flap their wings as though running in place from the sheer frustration of not being able to fly. Over time, the flapping became less as wings that cannot fly forget how. For Maximus "private" was, on one paw, sad and solitary; yet, on the other paw, with Wystan, private had been an intense closeness of feeling without words.

Huxley thought of some of his father's fellow senators who also would visit Trevenen's burrow. In the senate and out among the cat public, they seemed to be very different than when they were alone with his father. Conversely, Huxley's father seemed the same to Huxley wherever he was. As he was in private, he remained in public.

Maximus knew that the way he felt with Wystan was closer to how he felt with Trevenen than with other cats he met so far. And that to be alone with Trevenen in private was no different than being with Trevenen among other cats. Trevenen did not change and his calm, assuring face remained the same—always.

Gerald bemusedly watched the two kittens' eyes deep in thought; he could see that Maximus, the new student, was just as thoughtful as Huxley was. It was time to prod: "Time! What comes to your minds?"

Simultaneously, Huxley answered, "Father," and Maximus, "Trevenen."

Gerald's blue eyes grew even brighter still above his wide smile. "Today was a good lesson." And he left without another word.

A Month Later:

· · · · · · · · · · · · · · ·

The lush greenery on each side of the river was quite still on a windless day. The day before, Gerald in another lesson had Huxley and Maximus walk with him by the river. He walked carefully, using his long staff, which he said had been hewn from tree a struck by lightning and thus, was nearly white, and even more light from years in the sun. Then they sat on a large boulder right on the water's edge. "Now see," Gerald said, how the surface of the water is so still that you can see your reflection in it. All seems at peace, and perhaps this is so."

Maximus had never seen himself before and the first impression was startling. If one has never seen one's own face, indeed, it is strange. Before this moment of seeing his face for the first time, the voice and words that came from Max's head had not seemed related to the cat that said them. Nor could he see himself with others as he could now. Not only did he see his face but the faces of Huxley and Gerald as well. This was the first moment that he truly felt he was not separated from the world. Instead, for the first time, he felt that there was a "whole" to which he belonged. The feeling was a good one; it reminded him of the wholeness he felt under Wystan's wing. Max by now also knew that this was exactly how Gerald wanted him to feel. With Gerald as teacher, there were no coincidences. Max could also see how much larger he had grown than Huxley had though Huxley was older.

Gerald handed the staff to Max. "Now my strong young student, let us see what happens when you dip this staff a little into the water's surface." Max took the staff and was amazed at its weight and strength. Far more, he thought, than one would have imagined that Gerald's aged and thin frame could have managed. He dipped the staff a mere few inches into the water, and other than the initial small ripple that briefly disturbed their reflection, the water quickly reformed and they could see the perfect picture of themselves again.

Max was holding the staff without effort with one paw. Gerald motioned downward with his hand that Max should lower the staff further. Max did so quickly dropping it in a good three feet and the staff was nearly ripped from his one paw, so that he reached out the other to steady it. This time the disturbing ripple on the surface was wider and took longer to settle down, but with two paws holding fast, the still picture appeared once again.

Gerald motioned to drop the staff lower. This time Max had to stand in order to restrain the staff from the great rush of flowing water just below the calm surface, and no matter how hard he exerted his great strength, he could not still the staff, calm the water, nor see their reflections clearly any longer. Gerald motioned upward so Max could withdraw the staff and sit again. "Now my young students, what do we learn from this?"

Max was still catching his breath, so Huxley answered, "Look before you leap." Gerald laughed. He had never heard it put quite this way before and decided to save it for future reference

"Quite right, Huxley, or, more precisely, one must feel before he leaps. For in this instance, one cannot see. Nature is not easy! Sometimes it appears calm; sometimes it does not. At all times, however, nature lives with great energy and we must be aware of this. Even more so, when nature is disturbed, as we have done with the staff in the water, nature reacts. The greater we interfered with nature—that is, the lower we dropped the staff—the more disturbed nature became. Creatures are also natural, and one must know that a creature's calm appearance does not always tell what is in the creature's heart. And like the water, the more one disturbs a creature, the more it will react. Today was a good lesson. I do believe you could even continue doing well without Old Gerald."

The Next Morning
• • • • • • • • • • • • • • • • • •

Dawn arrived, and the first light opened the eyes of the yawning students. They waited for Gerald's long shadow to appear. Instead they saw a much smaller, fluttering shadow. Stephen the Sparrow entered the burrow instead of Gerald. His mind spoke: "Gerald sent me to tell you that he is needed urgently elsewhere." Maximus and Huxley were stunned, for they had become very fond of those blue eyes. Stephen said, "Don't look so sad. *I'm* still here."

The yellow sparrow was answered by more long yawns to which Stephen replied, "Your enthusiasm is overwhelming. I have a mind not to tell you of his gift." The kittens' yawning jaws closed quickly enough and they said in unison; "What is it?"

"It waits for you by the river at the great rock of yesterday's lesson."

Huxley and Max were puzzled. They had neither seen nor heard the petulant sparrow the day before; yet, he always seemed to know everything. Stephen knew their thoughts, giggled and flew out before any questions might be asked. The kittens ran just as quickly to the river. There, leaning against the rock, was Gerald's Staff. Indeed, Maximus and Huxley would share it, each in a way they would have never imagined.

Since they were now at the river, Maximus was reminded of yesterday's lesson and the strength of the water when the staff was lowered deeper into it. He had seen grown cats straddle the waters' edge, but only the very strongest and most confident attempted to swim across. This was risky as the river rushed to become a waterfall that landed on a bed of jagged rock far below. Maximus was bold and strode into the water slowly, gauging the speed of the water he felt at his feet. He removed his cape, threw it back to Huxley and went in the water to his waist. He braced his broad and strong body and measured the river's force. Max knew he could reach the other side. He stretched forward to dive in. Huxley and Stephen did not have enough time to stop him. Max made circles with his powerful front paws and cut through the rushing rapid as well or better than any adult cat had ever done. Of course, though he was still just an adolescent he was already as large or larger than a grown cat. He forged through the water and reached the farther shore. Pulling himself out and standing straight, he shook the river off his fur and then raised his paws in triumph. He yelled back to Huxley and Stephen, "I wish Trevenen and Gerald could have seen me!"

Unknown to Max this raised in Huxley's mind a feeling of competitiveness. He too would wish his father's approval. Max was built more for sports and seemed destined to become a warrior. Huxley was more of a thinker, more inward than Max, and certainly not as large and strong. His father was pleased at Max's physical ability and took care to praise the orphan who had no parents and needed reassurance. He was also proud of Huxley's intellect, believing he would take after his grandfather, the scientist. Trevenen would sometimes forget that his son was still missing his very doting mother and that his father needed to replace the approval she had given him so freely. At this moment Huxley's intellect gave in to his emotions. Impulsively, he jumped in, forgetting to remove his own cape. Whatever little chance he might have had without the cape, he had no chance with it. Huxley was no match for the water that weighted the cape and pulled it tight around his neck like a noose. He could not breathe and the rapid river carried him toward the falls.

Max's paws dropped in shock. He began running along the water's edge as fast as any cat in Catland could run. His mind told Stephen, "Fly to the burrow; get Trevenen's long rope." Max kept pace and could see Huxley at first flailing about but soon the caped cat was limp, unconscious. Max thought that the tiny sparrow could not manage that great coil of rope. He was wrong, for Stephen, of course, was no ordinary sparrow. Max saw that little streak of yellow flying faster than a falcon with that tiny beak carrying the rope that was a good twenty times larger than his little body. Max's mind called, "Stephen, fly to the great tree at the falls edge, tie the rope to that branch that stretches across and bring the other end back to the tree's trunk." The sparrow roared ahead and followed orders. Maximus was now running at a speed no other cat in history or legend had ever achieved. He leaped up the side of the great tree, and has he had done before when he saved Stephen from the crows, Maximus climbed vertically as if a giant spider. He reached Trevenen's rope and saw Huxley's inert form coming nearer. Max would swing across and grasp Huxley at the fall's edge. The timing had to be perfect. He took the rope in his paws, his heart beating to leap out of his mouth. He was not scared for himself. He was terrified for Huxley for he knew why his good friend had jumped in and Maximus blamed himself.

At this second, he heard Gerald: "Maximus! Close your eyes and think of me. When I say jump, do so—and I will do the rest. . . . Jump!!"

Maximus leaped off the tree and reached with his right front paw while his left held the rope fast. He splayed his claws wide so they would be a grappling hook. Eyes still closed, he felt himself grab at Huxley's cape. He took hold and swung the rest of the way across. He opened his eyes and landed square on his back legs. Gently, he put Huxley down and removed the cape from his neck. His friend was not moving. Max lifted him as a baby and cradled him in his great paws as Wystan had once done for him with his wing.

Stephen flew ahead to alert Trevenen who was in the senate. Huxley's father saw the sparrow darting frantically. He left his fellows and ran out of the council burrow. There was Maximus holding Huxley who was still motionless.

That Night:
• • • • • • • • • • •

Huxley was safe in his burrow but still unconscious. Trevenen and Maximus were curled on either side of Huxley to keep him warm. Christopher the Physician had just left after staying all day. He could offer no more than hope. Huxley had been under the water for a long time. Maximus told Trevenen what had happened. Max's grief was clear. Trevenen understood the issues concerned and felt his own blame. He did not admonish Maximus who needed no lesson nor reminder of what his impulsiveness had started. Trevenen knew Max was just being a young cat as was Huxley.

Huxley began to slowly regain consciousness but did not yet move. He thought he had opened his eyes, but he saw only dark shadows within shadows. He sensed that two of the shadows were his father and Maximus. They in turn saw the lids of Huxley's eyes raise a little and were overjoyed, calling his name. Huxley heard them and only his profound grogginess slowed the even more profound panic that was taking hold of him. He raised his right front paw to his right eye and felt if it, indeed, was open. It was. Then he pushed that paw a little forward, as would a cat in a cave with no light whatsoever. "Father, I cannot see!"

The Next Morning:
• • • • • • • • • • • • • • • • • •

"Huxley was in the water long enough" explained Christopher the Physician, "for a bacterial infection to get into his eye tissue. I have given him an herbal medication for his eyes and another to lessen his anxiety."

A nervous father asked, "When will his vision return?"

"Trevenen, my old and good friend, I wish I could comfort you, but you need truth. I don't know. It could be months or longer and it will be gradual." Christopher hesitated, and then continued, "But you must be prepared that if—and I am afraid I must say if it returns—it will never be normal."

"And what of his education; he so wished to become as my father, a scientist."

Christopher, who had the great scientist as his teacher and had, in turn, planned to teach the younger Huxley who was a brilliant young cat, could only shrug. In his heart, however, he knew that without clear sight, science and medicine would not be possible.

Just outside the burrow, Maximus heard all . . . and cried. Then, landing like a feather on his left shoulder, the tiny sparrow's mind spoke, not in Stephen's voice, but in Gerald's: "Maximus, there is much to do and your tears must end. Experience is learned backwards, but must be lived forwards. You cannot change what has been, but you must take charge of what will be."

Then the yellow sparrow flittered to the right shoulder and spoke again, now in Wystan's voice: "Come now, my first son, there is more than one way to be strong. The Great Mystery's gift of your large size and physical ability must be matched with an equally strong will to empower the mind as well. The mind, not the body, is the true source of strength and courage. Stephen the Sparrow has survived every natural catastrophe and every threatening creature with his wits, not his size. Remember this!"

Stephen returned to the other shoulder. In his own somewhat high, squeaky, teasing tone, the sparrow's mind said. "Well, I hope you were paying attention. Stop moping around and go take care of your best friend. There is still much for you two to learn and you, Maximus, are going to be both teacher and student."

Three months later:

Maximus and Huxley walked in the Huxley Meditation Gardens, named after the famous scientist. The sun was bright and the flowers were in full bloom with their colors alive and distinct. Maximus brought Huxley here to cheer him. Lately, Huxley was seeing colors and shapes again. Slowly, very slowly, there was improvement. Still, the near-blind young cat made good use of Gerald's staff to guide him. He walked well. One could not detect that he could not see until one was near enough to notice that Huxley's eyes did not quite focus on the face opposite him while his cat ears, shifted and turned sharply toward a voice, if not the face.

They sat on a stone bench. Maximus read to Huxley every single day from one of the many books that Gerald had listed in a syllabus before the wise old teacher had left Catland. (Or at least his body had left Catland. He otherwise seemed to be around to visit minds when a mind needed visiting.) Both young cats were older. Huxley was nearly fully-grown. Maximus was uniquely grown. Max was already a head taller and a paw broader than Trevenen who was himself one of the larger cats in Catland. The black-backed, white-chested cat was expanding at a rate that would make him a giant among the other cats. He was already Catland's leading athlete. So much so that he now declined many competitions because no one else could possibly win. He still accepted non-competitive events of speed and strength, particularly if he could influence younger kittens or raise sympathy and funds for a good cause. Max had been humbled by Huxley's accident. The Great Mystery gave him his gifts and he could not take them for granted. They were a blessing that did not belong to him alone. Trevenen had saved him and brought him to this place where Huxley was his great friend who loved him like a brother. Maximus was grateful to them and to Catland. Huxley never said a word about his lack of sight, never complained, never regretted. Maximus knew his physical strength could not match Huxley's mental courage.

Stephen the Sparrow hovered nearby, sometimes at so great a height, his yellow streak seemed one of the sun's sparkles. Other times he sat on a branch over their heads. Even with his high-silly voice that jested more than rested, the sparrow always gave his two young charges the impression that Stephen knew more than he said. Indeed, they believed that Gerald, and even Wystan the Wise, were always aware of their doings. This fact deterred any thought of slacking off from their studies. Max's large head made for a strong voice. He read from the *Book of Christopher* who is a philosopher as well as a physician:

The Book said: *One cannot know to look at creatures, which ones are Truly Weak or Truly Strong. The dinosaurs were the most powerful; yet, they are all gone. Who can say if those creatures that are now leaders will remain so, or if, in the future, leadership will mean the most wisdom or the most powerful? What comes, goes. The water flows, in, out, over, and around as long as there is rain. The body holds the mind; the mind flows even if the body is still. The will to think first, and from this deep thought then act wisely, for the many, is Truly Strong. To act with little or no thought, except for one's self, is Truly Weak. The Weak seek attention; the Strong pay attention. The Weak speak much and say little; the Strong speak little but say a great deal. The Weak wear a mask in public to hide what they fear in private; the Strong have one face in public and private. The Weak wish to act brave when there is no real need; the Strong are only brave when the need is real.*

Maximus said no more. He put his strong paw on his friend's shoulder, a silent message without words that was stronger than any sounds either could make. In this world of meditative silence is the place where the Great Mystery is best understood. Huxley purred, then Maximus. Stephen, overhead on a branch, heard them both and he was glad.

The quiet and solitude were soon accompanied by the mellow sound of the Horn of Welcome. Trevenen and the Freedom Riders were returning from another mission.

The Arrival of Princess Blue:

Trevenen and the Riders had ventured east to what would later be called the Orient. There, a rare breed of cats had once flourished. Alas, no longer. In the past, kinder humans—and one was Gerald—believed these cats to be Gods and protected them.

In recent times these humans were few and they had been pushed aside by the more unruly human tribes. The number of eastern cats had dwindled to a few. The cat senate, fearing the eastern cats would become history, sent the Riders to help them. Alas, Trevenen arrived a day too late. For whatever reason, and even though it seemed some cats had just been there judging from the sight of food and other evidence, no cats could be found, or so they thought. When the Riders searched a small burrow, there was, under a great pile of leaves, a tiny voice crying the saddest meows they had ever heard. Trevenen gently pawed aside a few leaves until he saw a pink ribbon (and he did not know pink, it was a color not of his experience or of any other cat from Catland). This odd color was atop a most tiny female kitten head, a head of light gray with streaks of charcoal. The little face, hearing the purring of other cats, bravely lifted its eyes to see if this were true. And now, Trevenen's shock at the color pink was nothing as when he first saw that her eyes were blue. He gasped and bade his fellow Riders forward quietly so as not to scare her. They, too, saw the blue eyes, and the six, in unison, stretched their paws forward and placed their great heads on them. In the Ancient History, the great first Gods of Catland had Blue Eyes. This lone survivor was a descendent of Cat Royalty, perhaps even from a direct line to the legendary Princess Blue, the first mother of the Great Mystery. She blinked those special eyes that only Gerald's could compare to. (This was also a clue to the great respect the Cats gave to Gerald.) Her fur was dirty and matted; yet, her little face revealed a great beauty, even as frightened and sad as it was. She seemed to know that she was the last of her kind. Trevenen carried her back to Catland.

There, Huxley and Maximus ran toward the Horn of Welcome. Indeed, as long as Huxley felt his friend next to him, he could still run as if sighted.

Smitten with a Kitten:

On the return from the east, the great warrior cats were entranced with their little kitten to whom they gave the name Princess Blue in honor of her first ancestor. They, with their great rough tongues, first dipped her carefully into clear rainwater and then, gently licked her fur clean and with their claws combed the fur to a shiny luster. Her fur was longer than theirs and stood up on her body at a rearward angle rather than stretched back close along the sides. The fur on her stomach was a mass of curls—and the Riders had never seen curly fur before. She herself had washed her pink ribbon and had also taken along with her a little box made from a black wood that would now be called ebony. The box contained odd little shapes of shiny stuff. Some were yellow like the sun; some were as the linings of great clouds where the sun would brighten edges to what is now called silver. These little shapes were hard. Sometimes she put them on her individual claws; others went on her ears—indeed, her ears had little holes for just this purpose. Such decorations were unknown to Catland, which was a very utilitarian place. Other than capes for rain, ropes for climbing, pulling, and tying, tools and weapons, the males and females of Catland knew little else, and nothing for the pure sake of decoration. In this, Princess Blue was a most incredulous sight. And her voice—her purring was continuous, as Maximus knew Wystan's to be, only the volume changed from soft to loud and back. Her meows were short, high-pitched little squeaks, and when she spoke, she was so delicate, with a flute-like tone that sounded like music—sometimes music that one would wish to dance to, or when she was sad in remembering her lost family, it became the wind's sigh at dusk and all who listened could not help but be quiet and thoughtful.

And those eyes—she was carried into Catland on Trevenen's back with her front paws around his neck as she looked past his right shoulder forward into the throng of cats that came to greet the returning warriors. The cats of Catland stopped in wonder in seeing the only other blue eyes they had seen besides Gerald's—and that pink ribbon—and her toes and ears! They were awed as she looked like the drawings in the *Book of the Great Mystery* of the first mother. They were also a little frightened and so was she. As the cats approached Trevenen, Princess Blue withdrew her head and nuzzled into the back of his wide neck. He said to her, "Fear not, little Princess, they will come to love you as we, the Riders, have come to love you for your sweetness." He then saw Maximus and Huxley bounding to the front of the assembly. Trevenen was pleased to see Huxley keep up with Max as if he could see just as well as he once had; yet, when the two reached Trevenen and Huxley let go of the edge of Max's cape, Huxley was not quite as sure and steady, at least until Max whispered into his ear and the sound became an anchor to which Huxley centered his spirit and found his sure stance again. With this assurance and Gerald's staff, one could only know by the most intense scrutiny that Huxley could not see.

Trevenen signaled for Maximus that he and Huxley should come to him and the duo preceded a pace to the leader of the Freedom Riders. They saw the little charcoal paws clinging under Trevenen's ears, but not much else as Princess Blue still buried her tiny face in the nape of her rescuer's neck. Trevenen said calmly to the little paws, "Be not afraid, for my two sons—one also adopted as you now are—are before us and you may trust them as you would trust Trevenen." (Trevenen considered Maximus as his son and would never call him his ward or refer to himself as any other but Max's father.)

Over his right shoulder rose the pink ribbon above and between the charcoal ears with their soft white stripes. The ribbon startled all that could see it, but not Huxley who didn't. A little squeak was heard and slowly the head lifted and became visible as did the second and even more amazing sight, those blue eyes again. There were renewed gasps from the inhabitants of Catland and Princess Blue shyly ducked her head down again.

Trevenen bade his sons come right up to his shoulder, and with his eyes signified that they should speak to welcome her.

Maximus said, in his deep voice that echoed around his enormous chest, "Greetings, I am Maximus, and I will be proud to be your friend."

His power was a bit intimidating, and she still hesitated. Maximus nudged Huxley, the gentler soul, whose voice was calm from the great internal well that was the inner silence he'd learned to love due to his blindness. With such softness, Huxley told her, "Indeed, little one, I am Huxley. Maximus and I welcome you and wish to show you the great peace and serenity that is Catland."

The voice reminded her of her teacher, whom she'd known only briefly before the terrible last days of her Kingdom. His name was Gerald. And just before Gerald was carried off by the enemy to who knows where, it was he who hid her under the pile of leaves while telling her not to come out until she heard cat voices. At the thought of that human's blue eyes and how Huxley's voice sounded like his, her head popped up again and she saw for the first time the sons of Trevenen.

There was the giant Maximus, whom Trevenen had described to her on the way home; he was even larger than she could have possibly imagined. And there was Huxley, with his soft eyes that while they could not see outward seemed to draw her inward into his gentleness. Princess Blue let go of Trevenen. She landed on her paws then rolled on her back to expose her precious chest and stomach of delicious curly ringlets.

She said to everyone's delight, "I'm a girly-girl with curly-curls," which is what she would say to her father and mother when she wanted attention.

Trevenen explained, "This means she wants you to rub her stomach; it is an Eastern version of a Floppy." So Huxley and Maximus tickled her tummy. And at the sight of her rolling from side to side and the sound of the little girl's happy giggles, the citizens of Catland joyously sang a round of sweet laughter along with the sound of their paws applauding. The princess was startled and leaped up into Max's great chest where she hid her face as he cradled her in his tree-sized limbs. The many cats stopped their appreciation. Then Huxley, with his voice that sounded like Gerald, said, "Be not afraid, Catland loves you and this is the sound of their love." Then her little head looked over at the crowd of cats, and Princess Blue's tiny mouth gave a little squeak. The cats applauded again. This time, she just enjoyed her happiness.

From this moment the inseparable duo of Huxley and Maximus became an inseparable trio with the addition of Princess Blue.

Three Months Later:
• • • • • • • • • • • • • • • • • • • •

Every morning, Princess Blue liked to go to the river's edge and the two young cats would accompany her. It was in reflections of water that she had learned to arrange her pink ribbon and to decide what little objects would emerge from her ebony box to adorn her paws and ears. She had the oddest walk. When she was on all fours, if one looked from behind, one could only see her very bushy tail, which hid her short legs and tiny body. This tail would seem to bounce up and down, yet also swish left and right at the same time. Huxley remarked that she seemed to hop rather than walk. If the princess stood up, she would be very straight as if balancing some object on her head and between her little ears. On this morning she chose to adorn her head with azure stones that she said had come from a great desert across an ocean to the west—or so Gerald had said when he gave them to her.

She had told Huxley and Maximus of Gerald and now they knew why he had left Catland, and this was to teach Princess

Blue. If so, and if Gerald had left them his books, then they would honor his wish and include her in their daily lessons. Like most kittens, she preferred to play, but when she could be made to sit still—for she was a most busy little Princess, running here, there and everywhere as she was curious about all of Catland and its inhabitants, she was very smart indeed. When she made her visits around Catland she won every single heart and it was no small thing that she had a great memory and could retain the details of every name in every Cat family that she met. Princess Blue seemed always to be really concerned with their lives and she was most ready to be helpful if a mother cat had too many newborn kittens and too little rest or if an elderly cat needed an errand run or if a sick cat wished company.

She was a Princess *of* the cats but never, never *over* them. In this short time, she learned well Gerald's lessons and though but a lass, grasped the philosophy of kindness that Gerald so wished that the Princess, Huxley, and Maximus should learn. For Gerald knew that in the eternal plan of the Great Mystery, they would be the future leaders of Catland. And no doubt, all three were greatly concerned as to what had happened to Gerald. Maximus was afraid that he was now in that terrible cave along side Wystan the Wise. Someday Max would go and rescue them as Trevenen had rescued him.

A year later:

••••••••••••

Huxley and Maximus were now nearly adult cats in age and size. Of course Max had been large for a long time and was now two heads taller and one shoulder wider than any other cat ever seen. Maximus was training to be a Freedom Rider—his great athleticism took to the martial arts lessons with ease. Huxley's vision had improved so that he could now see the outline of any creature and his inner eye filled in the centers of those outlines with their shapes. Indeed, his night vision seemed even better than before his eyes were afflicted. Huxley also wanted to be a Freedom Rider, but his father, Trevenen, fearing for his son's not quite right vision, wouldn't allow it. Instead, he was teaching Huxley the ways and laws of the Cat Senate so that one day he might take Trevenen's seat on the Cat Council. Huxley's disappointment was great at not being allowed to join the Freedom Riders. He was already disappointed that he could never become a scientist like his grandfather.

Huxley and Maximus had always talked of the day when they would go together to rescue Wystan the Wise and now perhaps Gerald too as who knew where the humans had taken him. Maximus felt his best friend's sadness and secretly taught him the lessons of Rider training that he himself had learned. Huxley learned quickly and his other senses were doubly acute to compensate for his eyes—he could hear the slightest sounds at twice the distance than could Maximus, and his cat nose, by its nature as with any cat was very sensitive as it twitched in detection, and could snare the faintest scent carried on the lightest wind. These sharper senses could be—and would be— a great advantage in the near future.

Princess Blue was still quite small in size but her stature in and out of Catland had grown. She was the Great Mystery's instrument of divine kindness to all creatures, even Stephen, despite his whiny, high-pitched bossiness. She understood he meant well and could forgive him anything for he knew Gerald. Some of the other young female cats were most enthralled with Blue's ribbons and shiny objects and she would share them and teach them how to make their own. The Princess delighted everyone with her squeaky giggles and hopping about. She arrived everywhere as if she were a chorus of singers and cast of dancers all in her little self. When she was not laughing, her voice was so serene and a soft tonic for the sad, lonely, and sick. One could not fail to purr in her presence—and she, well, she never stopped purring and did so even in her sleep. She'd curl up and one could only see her fluffy fur, but the sound of the continuous purring always made any cat near her think of the Great Mystery and peace. Hence, Huxley and Maximus felt peaceful a good deal of the time.

On this morning, just after dawn, she hopped to the river to see her reflection and choose what objects from her ebony box (always looped by a cord over her left shoulder), to wear as she looked at her reflection in the water. She was at the water's edge and stared but not at her own face. Instead she saw Gerald's face in the water. This caused her to hop up and backwards as if jerked by one of Max's great ropes. The princess nosed her way again to the edge and looked over.

Gerald was still there and his face said so that only her mind could hear, "It is time!" Then the water rippled and Gerald was gone and she saw her own blue-eyed face—but not for long. She turned around and her short little legs carried her as fast as they could to find Maximus and Huxley.

She knew of their secret place in the deep woods where Maximus taught Huxley how to be a Freedom Rider. Huxley scented her approach long before Maximus did and could tell by the speed of her fast closing sweetness that she was running. Huxley said strongly to Maximus, "Come!" Maximus knew not to doubt Huxley's nose or ears and they ran together to meet the Princess.

Out of breath, she told them what had happened at the river.

All three sat on a fallen tree under an umbrella of other limbs and leaves still upright through which the sun peaked making lines of brightness over them. The three were silent, wondering what Gerald meant by "It is time!"

The Princess spoke first. "We must rescue him!"

"Yet," Maximus wondered, "where is he?"

Above them a leaf fluttered down on Huxley's head and then more leaves upon the three of them. It could only be Stephen.

Huxley, without looking up, called, "I see, dear Stephen that you wish to get our attention." Then the tiny yellow sparrow himself floated down and landed on Max's shoulder, gripping his tiny feet into the thick rope that always rested there.

The three said together anxiously, "Well?"

Then in the voice of Wystan the Wise Stephen said, "It is time, and you know where we are."

And now they did. The awful cave in the horseshoe plateau.

Max's head turned left and right and he said to Huxley and Princess, "Wystan has spoken; he and Gerald are waiting for us."

Huxley answered, "We must go to my father."

The quartet double-stepped (and Stephen double-winged) to the senate where the Cat Council was in session.

They entered the Circle of Wisdom, which had been built from the great rocks near the river many years ago atop the peak of Cat Valley's highest hill. Trevenen was speaking to the Senators:

"Our frontier scouts have received news from some of the border merchants that there may be Cats held in the distant city of Nilreb, which is an outpost on the edge of the Endless Lake across from which are the humans of the west, and it is there that the leader Reltih trades with his western counterparts." Trevenen had not given up on finding Maria and he could not bring himself to dismiss even the slightest rumor. "The Freedom Riders are ready to leave before sundown; what say you Council?"

The Council agreed and this session was over.

Huxley said to Maximus, "This complicates matters."

He was right. When they told his father of Wystan and Gerald, Trevenen was very concerned; yet, he said that their rescue would have to be the next mission after the raid on Nilreb. Huxley and Maximus knew the Riders might not be back for a month and who knew what could happen in that long a time. Gerald and Wystan did not send mind messages without good cause. Trevenen would not be deterred and Huxley knew why—the search for his mother. With a gesture Huxley bade

Maximus and the Princess desist from pleading, and they left the Circle of Wisdom.

Although Princess Blue did not speak, her blue eyes were very, very sad, for not only did she miss Gerald, he was the last link to the family and country she had lost.

Maximus could not bear her sadness, which was so opposed to her normal happiness. With his great red cape billowing in a summer wind and his long ropes circled around each shoulder, he stood to his full and very great height.

"Then *I* will go for them. I remember how to get there."

Princess Blue knew he was doing it for her. "No Maximus, you cannot go alone, I would be so afraid for you. I will come too."

Huxley and Maximus knew this was impossible for both would then be doubly afraid for her sake as her short little legs could never run as fast as Maximus could and Max would very likely need to run very fast. There was only one alternative and Huxley gave it. "Fear not little Princess, I will go with Maximus."

Then Stephen spoke up. "And I will go too, Princess, as their scout. I can fly ahead and tell them what they will find."

Now the Princess seemed less sad and this alone inspired Huxley and Maximus, for truth be told, the love they had for her as a little friend was now something else. Now they were both *in love* with *her*, the beautiful Princess Blue.

It was agreed, and they would also leave before sundown, as would the official Freedom Riders—although a minute or two after Trevenen did.

Dusk that evening:
● ● ● ● ● ● ● ● ● ● ● ● ● ● ● ● ●

Huxley, Maximus, and Princess Blue bid their heartfelt farewells to Trevenen and the other Freedom Riders while their own hearts beat fast at the mission they had set for themselves.

When Trevenen and the Riders had crossed the river and disappeared in the evening mist, Huxley, Maximus, and Stephen also prepared to depart.

The Princess cried and squeaked and hugged her elder friends (and even kissed Stephen while the sparrow chattered non-stop). She begged that they be sooooooooooo careful. Then, under the cover of darkness, off they went.

A week later:
● ● ● ● ● ● ● ● ● ● ●

Trevenen and the Riders returned much earlier than expected. On the way, a reliable cat scout informed him that there were no longer any Cats in Nilreb if there had ever been any at all. The mission was pointless and what was to have been a month-long trek ended abruptly. Trevenen's sadness over Maria continued.

Trevenen returned to Catland. He looked all over and inquired as to where Huxley and Maximus were. Puzzled cat citizens were now just realizing that no one had seen them for a while. Huxley's father sent for Princess Blue. She slowly entered his burrow instead of hopping in quickly as was her normal pace. This was sign enough that something was up.

"Where are Huxley and Maximus? No one has seen them and all are surprised to see you *not* with them."

The Princess crouched low to the ground, a cat sign that meant she was in trouble. Trevenen crossed his paws over his chest and assumed a most stern demeanor.

"I am waiting."

The Princess tried a distraction. She threw herself on her back, legs up, tummy exposed. "I'm a girly girl with curly curls." But from her now upside down glance at Trevenen, she could see that it wasn't going to work this time. He didn't flinch an inch, nor did the slightest amusement appear on his face. She resumed her crouching position and, avoiding eye contact, she confessed. "They have gone to rescue Wystan and Gerald."

Trevenen had feared this and now it was true. He asked her, "How long?"

She answered, "Right after you left for Nilreb."

The Frontier beyond Catland:
• •

Maximus had forgotten how little he was when Trevenen rescued him and how much of the trip he spent in a sack over Trevenen's shoulder. Therefore, it was a good thing that Stephen was with them for Max actually remembered almost nothing and Huxley had never before been too far from Catland at all. Both cats were astounded by the number and sounds of so many diverse creatures from earth and sky that they'd never seen or heard before. And the creatures they met were just as curious. They had seen cats before but never one like Maximus.

At first, they stood off along the trail or hovered over them. There was one who today would be called an elephant, and just as today, he was the biggest of land creatures. There were horses, but, unlike today they were merely the size of a very large dog. Stephen conversed with all of them with his mind and Maximus listened in and it seemed as if the sparrow knew every single one of them. Stephen particularly flew along side a hawk. Many birds visited with them, yet none looked like Wystan, and Maximus asked Stephen if there were others like Wystan.

"Yes, many, they are in Eagleland, but since Wystan was taken captive no one has seen or heard from them. He is their leader and they are lost without him."

Huxley said, "Perhaps, they need him most now and this is the reason for his summons."

Stephen did not answer and Huxley and Maximus always thought that the little sparrow knew much more than he ever let on. The creatures kept them company on their journey and seemed to have an extra bit of jauntiness to their strides that had been less evident when they were first seen. The birds swooped and looped and sang happy songs.

Stephen perched on Max's shoulder and said, "They sing for us Maximus, for they know what we are going to do and they are glad."

"Why so, Stephen?"

The sparrow flew off without responding. Huxley admonished him, "You are such a tease, Stephen."

And all of the creatures laughed as if sharing some great secret.

That night they camped under an arbor of tall trees and the caress of summer breezes moved the leaves and their sound whispered them to sleep. When morning came, they woke and all of the creatures had left them.

Stephen answered their unspoken question. "Yes, we are nearing our destination and the creatures are afraid to be any closer."

They arose and continued their journey. The sparrow, while giving directions, flew ahead to scout the enemy stronghold. He returned by early afternoon. "I have confirmed what our friend the hawk told me of the stronghold. He is able to fly so high that there is no chance of his capture and he informs the other creatures of their doings, particularly if there are packs of humans that are out looking for victims. He told me that since Trevenen's raid that brought Maximus to Catland, Reltih's forces have concentrated their defenses at night by having more scouts out and about and by building more fires in order to see better if anything approaches." Then Stephen paused. "However, as I have just confirmed with my own eyes, they are now not nearly so careful during the day. This is your best chance, but we must have a plan and it must be fast for while their daytime carelessness will help you get into the horseshoe stronghold, there will be little chance of their not seeing you when you seek to enter the terrible cave."

"But how," Huxley wondered, "can we do this in daylight?"

Stephen giggled, "Our bird friends suggested a plan before they departed."

Dawn, the Next Morning:
• •

The enemy guards were not up to serious guarding so early in the day. Snoozing was more like it. After all, who would dare try anything during the day? Stephen had observed that most of the guards were at the narrow entrance into the plateau and only a few were in front of the terrible cave. Some guards were atop the plateau, ready to toss rocks down, but not so many as would be there at night.

The sleepy sentries were aroused from their groggy early morning fog by the whoops and whistles of numerous high-flying birds, including Stephen's friend the hawk.

This air-born squadron mainly hovered over the stronghold's entrance. The terrible cave was at the back of the horseshoe and far from the opening, which was, of course, deliberate. Sometimes the birds would swoop down so that the guards and other humans who were now interrupted from their sleep were both cursing them but also fascinated by their sudden appearance over this place they otherwise avoided. Some shot arrows but the birds were too quick and since the birds were not being sneaked up on as in the past by the outlaws, they were more than able to avoid being hit.

More of the outlaws gathered under the birds as if this was a game—shooting arrows and throwing rocks at them but without success.

Over them, now unseen as the guards were distracted at the entrance by the flying birds, Maximus and Huxley had scaled the outer wall of the plateau just above where the terrible cave lay at the inner base. Bushes hid the cats. Maximus took one of the long ropes off his shoulder and tied one end to the base of a thick and strong tree trunk. Then Stephen, as he had done the day when Max (and Gerald) had rescued Huxley from the rushing river, flew across to the other side of the plateau and tied the other end of the rope to an equally strong tree there. None of the distracted outlaws saw the rope fly over so high above them where it looked like merely a thin hair from the ground. Stephen returned and reported that there were no sentries in the vicinity of where he'd tied the rope.

The plan was for Huxley to traverse the rope to the other side while the birds distracted the humans. Once on the other side, at Stephen's signal, Huxley would swing ever so dramatically across the stronghold to the other side drawing the enemy to him so that they would then climb up the side of the plateau after him. As they did this, Maximus would go down to the terrible cave for Wystan and Gerald and quickly return to Huxley's side. Then they'd descend the outer wall of the stronghold and escape. Time would be short, and there could be no delays or Huxley and his poor vision would be left to face the enemy alone.

Huxley made his way across unseen by the foolish humans who were still trying to shoot the birds with their wayward arrows. He traveled by pulling himself along with his four paws as he had been taught to do by Maximus. He reached the other side, untied the rope at his end, and waited. The sparrow flew toward Huxley and this was the sign for the last stage of the rescue to begin. Holding the rope in his front paws he made a running start and jumped off the edge of the plateau. He was now a tan pendulum swinging low and just above the humans who finally noticed something other than the birds. Huxley's down swing reached the bottom of its descent and his ascent to the other half of the plateau took him to the upper inside wall where he leaped to from his rope, landed on the steep incline, and dug in with his claws. Huxley climbed to the top of the plateau. Arrows followed him but none hit the moving target. A band of the enemy climbed after Huxley, and as they did Maximus stealthily clambered down to the terrible cave. He knew he must move quickly before the humans reached Huxley.

The cave was lit with torches and everything was dancing shadows. He came upon four guards. They feared the cats that were normal size, let alone Maximus who was much larger than normal. Two guards ran backwards at the first sight of him. The other two hesitated and began to draw their swords.

Maximus extended his front arms and splayed his great claws, each of which was longer than a big man's hand. The two dropped their swords, which were as nothing compared to the six blades Maximus displayed in each paw and joined their cowering fellows who shuddered and hid in the back of the cave.

There was only one cage left in the cave and Wystan was in it. The red-plumed eagle raised his head from between his wings. He was gaunt and looked weak of body; still, his great eyes were alive as no other eyes other than Gerald's had ever been so alive.

Maximus reached him and said, "I have come for you my first father."

The eagle answered, "As I knew you would my first son."

Maximus asked, "Where is Gerald? Was he not brought here as well?"

Wystan chuckled. "Gerald goes only where he wishes to go and this cave was not his wish. He is keeping busy in good works I assure you."

The cage was wrapped and tied by dozens of ropes with even more knots. Maximus could pull the wooden bars apart with his strength but was afraid of hurting Wystan. The giant cat began swiping the ropes with his sharp claws. There were too many and it was taking too long. Wystan's mind told Maximus to step back. The eagle raised his right wing and the hundreds of knots unraveled in seconds. The cage door opened and Wystan stepped out. Maximus did not understand. "My first father, why did you not free yourself long ago?"

Wystan shrugged his wings. "Because that is not how the story is to be told."

The eagle tried to take some more steps but could not, overcome by the years of inactivity and stumbled into Max's arms. "I cannot walk and certainly cannot fly."

Maximus gently picked up Wystan and had him sit upon a giant shoulder. Now he must return to Huxley before his friend had to flee the oncoming enemy and fend for himself in the darkness. With Wystan immobile, this would slow Max's ascent back up to the top of the plateau.

Up there, Huxley waited. The humans were almost over the edge to the top of the plateau and the near-blind cat had to decide if he should flee or fight. He would not go off without Maximus. He would fight. He heard the enemy before he saw them, and what he saw was very little more than dark shapes. He was not sure how many. He concentrated his other senses to hear and smell them. He knew by the sound of their feet in the dirt and their scent on his nose when they were close. He did not see them so much as feel them and they became visible in his mind's eye. Their arms wielded weapons and as they waved them Huxley detected the movement of air. He struck out and dropped one, then another with lightning blows. There were more. He felled them as they came, but they were coming too quickly. He would not flee and braced for the worst. A dozen charged at once—too many for any one cat besides Maximus and perhaps one other cat warrior.

Then from behind Huxley came a roar that only a father could make to defend his son. It was Trevenen.

The Freedom Rider's mighty blow dispatched with three guards at once and the other nine fell back. As they did, Maximus leapt over them with Wystan on his neck. Now the three cats were side by side, the giant Maximus in the middle. Seeing Max and Wystan, Trevenen said, "I see you have accomplished your mission. Valor is no longer required and retreat the better plan." Down they went on the outer wall of the plateau while the enemy was now afraid to continue following them out in the open field.

Trevenen stopped and faced his son and adopted son. "I should be very angry."

They did not answer.

"I should be, but I find this impossible when I look into the ancient eyes of this great eagle who saved Maximus so long ago." This was true; one could never feel less than positive emotions in Wystan's company. Wystan himself learned this ability to evince calm and goodwill from a long-ago human even older than Gerald. This was Charles of William who had descended with doves from the Great Mystery. He had been Wystan and Gerald's first teacher. Trevenen reminded Wystan of Charles.

Wystan nodded at Trevenen and his mind spoke, "Yes, noble warrior, do not be cross. Huxley and Maximus listened to their hearts and heard me call for them. They could do no other than to come."

Trevenen turned to Huxley. "You fought well and no doubt," now he looked at Maximus, "have had lessons in the martial arts, even if not from your father."

Maximus looked anywhere but at Trevenen. But then the leader of Catland touched the heads of both of his sons with his front paws and the younger cats knew that all was well and forgiven. Yet, there was still one concern to be remedied. Wystan could not walk, let alone fly, and Eagleland was a great distance away. He could not be left alone for he would only be captured again—or worse.

Maximus spoke. "Wystan cannot fly. I must carry him back to Eagleland."

Huxley looked at his best friend, then his father, and then he thought of Princess Blue. He missed her; they both did. Huxley was torn by two loyalties, to complete the rescue of Wystan or to return to Catland and see Princess again. He asked his father how she was.

"She is distraught with worry about both of you. She did keep her secret until I pressed her for your whereabouts. Meanwhile Blue does her enchantment throughout Catland. In her presence the sick feel almost cured; the grieving relieved, and orphan children unafraid. She was destined to come to Catland just as the Mystery required that you must rescue the red-plumed eagle."

Wystan said to Trevenen from atop Max's shoulder. "As for me, I can manage on my own."

Maximus would not hear of it. "I will not leave you until you are safe in Eagleland." And then Max said to Huxley and

Trevenen. "I will carry Wystan home and both of you should also return home. Catland should not be without its leader and his son for too long. Nor should we let the Princess continue to worry."

Wystan agreed. "The Princess should always have her mind free from worry so she can fill it with the love she gives wherever she goes." It was settled. Wystan and Maximus would go west to Eagleland and Trevenen, Huxley, and Stephen back to Catland.

How an Empty Cage Filled with Rage

Reltih the terrible was red with an anger that made his face seem to jump out from the long black hair that hung over the top of his black cape. He struck one guard, then the second, and down the line he slapped each of the fools who had allowed Wystan to escape, and to each one he said, "How many cats were there in the cave?" And when they would say, "One," he would hit each again. Some would dare to say, "but he was a giant and his claws were swords."

To which Reltih would bellow, "Then why are you not dead instead of standing here? Why are you all standing here while Wystan the Wise is gone?"

No answer.

He answered for them. "Because you did not fight. You should have been more afraid of me than this so-called giant with the white chest and red cape." He raised his fist again but stayed his hand when his second in command approached.

Elegnam whispered in Reltih's ear. "If you kill them all, no one will work for us anymore, and we will have to carry what we steal ourselves." Reltih looked at Elegnam and understood. Then he lowered his arm and told the fearful mob to get out of his sight.

One terrified guard said to another, "When Reltih is here, he is our worst fear. But if that giant ever comes again, I will still run and take my chances with Reltih later." Both shuddered at the thought of facing either.

Reltih walked with Elegnam and they spoke of this setback. Reltih said that now the master plan for conquest was disrupted. In due time the alignment of the Second Nature would be most propitious for the forces against the First Nature of the Great Mystery to achieve more power. Wystan was to have been the prize, a gift to the unseen evil force that is the Second Nature. Wystan's wisdom would have been transferred to this evil and turned into even stronger evil.

A Journey of Magic and Lessons

The four rescuers and the one rescued made their goodbyes. Huxley, Trevenen, and Stephen would return to Catland. Maximus would carry Wystan to Eagleland. This would take the giant cat into new lands just as the rescue mission had done. Truly, these were his first real travels away from Catland. Maximus had been fascinated by the great variety of sights, sounds, and wonderful new creatures he had met and seen. There would be more amazement.

Maximus asked his first father, "What now?"

Wystan's right wing pointed to the sun and the horizon line just below the sun. "There, where you see a faint, dark peak edging up from the line that meets land and sky, that is where we must go."

Maximus observed that this bleak peak was alone in its darkness while surrounded by vibrant and diverse shades of blues, greens, and browns as if this solitary landmark was a wound in an otherwise happy tapestry of light. He asked, "Does Eagleland lie beyond that one dark point?"

"No, Maximus, that one dark point is Eagleland. And now is the time Wystan must return before that darkness becomes permanent and Eagleland disappears forever."

Maximus thought of how the great red-plumed eagle's mind had untied the knots. "Wystan, there is something I do not understand."

"And what is that my first son?"

"If you could have freed yourself at any time, why didn't you?"

"I didn't because the Great Mystery does not see time as earth-bound creatures do. Time is an idea made up by creatures so that they may know how to measure space and distance. For example, when Trevenen, Huxley, and Stephen left us, Huxley asked me how long it might take for you to return to Catland. I answered two moons, after which he would have cause to worry if you did not return in that time, and no doubt, being your best friend, he would come looking for you. Yet, if no one ever left anyone, there would be no need to measure the separation and the idea of time might not have come to exist."

Maximus rubbed his chin with his giant paw. "I can understand what you say, but this does not explain why you did not free yourself sooner."

Wystan the Wise smiled the smile of a great knowing and of knowledge that neither Maximus nor few other creatures other than the eagle, Gerald and the Chosen Ones knew.

"Maximus, only the invented sense of time determines what is free or not free. In a manner of speaking, I appeared not to be free. Yet, this is only if one limits one's vision to what is seen instead of imagining what is felt by the spirit that is independent of the body. Our spirits enter newly born bodies and for the duration of this body, one imagines that the body can be captured and thus the spirit is captured too. Not so, if the spirit enters a body and then later leaves a body to return to the Great Mystery, has this spirit ever *not been free*? This body of an eagle called Wystan is not the essence of Wystan, which is the spirit of Wystan. When my body remained in the cage, my spirit was elsewhere and had no sense of time, as the body knows time. When the spirit meditates on the Great Mystery, there is no separation of space and distance, and time stops so that all moments exist as they were meant to, simultaneously, as if a giant painting within which all events appear at once."

Maximus considered this idea of a giant painting and then asked, "So then Wystan, if it were possible for a creature to stand back far enough, one could see all of time as one big picture without yesterdays, todays, or tomorrows?"

"Exactly, Maximus. Hence, my body may have been in one place for what seemed a measurable duration based on the limited vision of earth-bound creatures, but my spirit knew no such restrictions and was as free as it had always been."

"Nonetheless, wouldn't your body and your spirit have been freer somewhere else."

"Perhaps, but then I could not have rescued you so that you could later rescue me."

Maximus was about to interject another "but," when he realized that this circle of wisdom seemed to have no end—and this was exactly Wystan's point: there is no beginning or end—just an eternal *now*.

In the distance, they could see lightning and hear thunder. The very strange thing was that this lightning was not seen over the whole far-off sky, but only over the dark peak towards which the cat and eagle were headed. This was puzzling to Maximus as it seemed that the blight of that black spot was being singled out for a particularly angry attack by nature while being surrounded by sunshine and blue sky on either side. Indeed, a gigantic rainbow rose from the far left and far right of the dark peak and made a semicircle with only the apogee of its height hidden by the dry storm over the sad center. This was a strange storm because even with all of the blinding lightning and deafening thunder, there was no rain.

At the sight of the rainbow, Wystan said from his perch on Max's shoulder, "We must hurry—the rainbow warns me that we must hasten to the peak."

"Why?"

Wystan did not answer, but only moved to the middle of the back of Max's neck and reached around the front with his two wings, holding very firmly. "It is time for you to go on all fours Maximus and run with the speed no other creature can."

And in a blur the white chest, black-topped head, and red-caped back became a streak of color moving so fast that one could just see the blur of color but not the actual movement of the four legs.

Miles became moments until they reached the foot of the peak with Wystan's scarlet plume aflutter from the wind. Max's head had been down for the furious run and now looked up. He had never seen such a sight. The peak was black with dead vegetation and the soil itself gray as if the ashes of a long dead fire. Trees were black with not a single sign of a leaf signifying the slightest life. They climbed to the top and saw below a riverbed that split the bleak peak but not a hint that any rain had fallen upon the river's bed for years. On the other side of the dry riverbed there were more trees with twisted branches curling over and over upon themselves so that they blocked out any light to be seen from behind them. One only saw the blackness like the dead stillness of a moonless and starless night or the back of a fire-less cave. Before this day Maximus had only known the lush and verdant beauty of Catland and could have never imagined that nature could be so cruel.

"Wystan, where are we?"

Wystan was now atop Max's head. He did not answer. Instead, with a slow and great sweep, he raised his right wing to the sky right over the peak. The dark cloud directly above began to whirl rapidly becoming a vortex with a giant spin. The lightning and thunder became even more terrible and then from the whirling center of the vortex a flood of water was released in a torrent as though a rush from a collapsed dam. The torrent landed precisely in the dried riverbed with not a drop to either side, filling it in seconds instead of the hours that would have otherwise been needed by even the greatest storm. The water rushed through the valley.

Wystan then raised his left wing and the river's now full breadth overran the sides and bathed the dead vegetation. Wystan raised his right wing again and to the right of them, in only the time it took Maximus to gasp, the dead vegetation was fed with the magic of life and bloomed again in vibrant color and fullness. Wystan raised his left wing and this miracle was repeated to the other side. Then the great eagle raised both of his wings and pointed them towards those dense and light-preventing black trees. The water defied gravity and climbed up the thick and tall dead-gray trunks and turned them a living brown. The branches uncurled and straightened, then lush, green leaves appeared. Light now came through the straightened limbs.

Maximus saw some slight stirring in the brand new leaves of the trees and then a voice came from the trees loud enough to wake mountains.

"It is Wystan!"

And the eyes of Maximus were then filled with the sight of thousands of eagles flying out from the once-dead trees back into their renewed lives—their leader was home again!

The eagles formed a magnificent circle of which Wystan was the center and flew around him singing for joy.

Even with their joy, they would have normally been wary of the giant cat if not that Wystan sat on his shoulder. When Wystan told the story of the terrible cave and that Maximus had brought him home, the cat became their hero as well and would now forever be a great figure in the history of Eagleland

Later that night after the many eagles were exhausted from their happiness and had returned to sleep in the rejuvenated trees. Maximus and Wystan sat on a rock under a bright full moon and dancing stars.

"Wystan, it is a good thing to see the eagles so happy again. Yet, I must wonder why they were trapped in darkness until your return if you could have freed yourself sooner."

"Before I left, Eagleland was a most fortunate place as it is now—virtually all of these eagles were born into plenty and wanted for nothing. No effort was ever needed; hence, there was no sense of comparison. They became lazy, not just of body but also of mind—their collective spirit and their ability to meditate upon the Great Mystery had also nearly disappeared. While the collective body of Eagleland was full and fat, the collective mind was dying into apathy and ignorance. Soon, Eagleland would have been soulless, and without soul there would have been no progress towards the path of the Great Mystery—and that is much more important than being fat and full. Without knowing that there is dark, one cannot truly appreciate the light and think about why the light and dark need to be compared. Light and Dark, Strong and Weak, Good and Evil have no meaning without contrast and it is from thinking on their meanings that the collective mind moves towards the Great Mystery. The sages call this the Reconciliation of Opposites. The friction and fission of these opposites rubbing against themselves create the energy needed to learn about the Great Mystery. Without a Reconciliation of Opposites the body may be satisfied but the spirit knows nothing of what it means to be good, to be strong, to be heroic and noble. And without this knowledge life has no meaning. Moreover, the Reconciliation of Opposites explains the force of the First and Second Natures. The First Nature is the yearning for the Good Path of Upward Transcendence, the desire to move towards the love of the Great Mystery. The Second Nature is when one thinks too much of one's self and not for the good of the whole. Then one moves away from the Good Path towards Downward Transcendence. Yet, the great Mystery has determined that there *should* be two paths. If all Good is given instead of chosen, there would be no effort to learn the difference and no progress towards the evolution of consciousness."

Maximus was now beginning to see a bigger picture that became clearer with Wystan's words. Maximus had always had an intuition that there was something more than this earth but had heretofore not thought of it deeply. "Wystan, when you have thoughts such as these, is this what is meant when you say the word meditate?"

"Not quite my first son, but such thoughts guide one towards meditation." Then with his right wing Wystan pointed up to the bright full moon and then swept his wing across the sky. "There, far above us, the lights of the beautiful moon and the twinkling stars, even in all their magnificence, are just a mere fraction of the Great Mystery. Focus your eyes on them and imagine then how immense is that Mystery that is our guide to the spirit's eternity. Do so and you will see that your mind will move towards that feeling called meditation."

Maximus did so and soon his face held the sweetest smile.

On this very night Huxley and the Princess gazed at the same full moon, as did Maximus and Wystan. She said, "I wonder what Maximus is doing right now."

Max's great friend Huxley laughed and replied, "No doubt sitting as we are and wondering what *we* are doing."

Huxley and Princess were sitting on a rock at the river's edge. Her pink bow caught the moonlight and her blue eyes always shined in light or dark. Maximus had been gone for a full moon—the first time since the black-backed cat had come to Catland that he and Huxley had ever been separated for more than a few moments.

Princess asked Huxley, "How is that new device that sits on your nose?"

That day Christopher the Physician had given Huxley his latest invention—one made just for the cat with the poor eyesight. Christopher called them lunettes and they were what one now calls glasses. Indeed, they had improved Huxley's vision. Now the mere outlines he saw had filled in somewhat to assume shapes and he could see further than before—across the river even—the best surprise of these lunettes was that, if he held pages right up to his eyes, he could read on his own again. Up until today, with Maximus gone, Princess had been reading to him. She was glad of Huxley's ability to now read on his own even though she had rather enjoyed that he had depended on her. This was her nature—to help those who needed her most. Maximus was so great and strong that she could not help but think he needed help the least.

Today she had read to Huxley from *The Poems of Wystan* and then from *The Philosophy of Gerald*. These were books for deep thinkers and Huxley's years of near blindness had internalized much of his thought into introspection and he was becoming the most profound scholar in Catland. She loved to read to him—and he would instantly memorize the words, consider their meanings, and then speak of them with such sensitivity, interpreting the great love that Wystan and Gerald meant to share. As Huxley got older, his voice, the voice she first heard that sounded like Gerald, just became more like Gerald. Huxley's voice was a sweet, tenor voice of great clarity and much timbre—Huxley, even when speaking softly, sounded as if he were the clear echo of a great cave. Thus, his words seemed imbued with a sense of eternity as befit the destiny he as yet knew nothing about.

He said to her. "I miss him as if he were my real brother and not just my best friend."

"And I too—it seems odd for us not to be a trio."

"But is it," he replied, "all right that we are a duo."

The princess put her head on his chest and took his paw in her paw that was bejeweled with her trinkets. This was answer enough.

Maximus gave his farewell to Wystan and the eagles of Eagleland. "Perhaps," he said to Wystan, "in time you will even fly again."

"If it is meant to be, I will."

A flying cordon of a thousand eagles escorted Maximus to the border of their now once-again beautiful land. Wystan was still on the cat's shoulder and said in his ear, "Though my body will remain here, I will always be with you as will the love of these eagles. You will never be alone."

Then two senior eagles carried Wystan back to the great trees and as they did, Maximus heard the wise one's mind say to his mind, "Goodbye, my first son."

Maximus waved his great paw as his mind answered, "Goodbye, my first father."

The journey home was a thoughtful one for Maximus. He considered the Great Mystery and at night he would gaze upon the moon and stars and meditate upon the Mystery even more so. As he did, his concentration improved and his focus on the inner light as reflected in the night sky became stronger. Sometimes, even if just for a fleeting instant, he could feel that he was not Maximus, a creature distinct and separate, but one with Huxley, and Princess, and Wystan, and Gerald, and Trevenen, and Catland, and Eagleland, and the man in the moon that returned his gaze, and the stars that danced to the same inner music that he now felt.

Then he fell into a most beautiful and peaceful sleep and in his dreams he and Huxley and Princess were still kittens, playing by the river.

Part Two:

Ten years later:
● ● ● ● ● ● ● ● ● ● ● ● ●

Outside the great Cat Council a boy cat played with a rope given to him by his uncle who was not really his uncle but the best friend of his father so he was called uncle nonetheless. The kitten, Matthias had his father's coloring—a reddish tan mixed in with stripes of off-white. The red contrasted with the color of the boy cat's eyes that came from his mother—a brilliant blue. Inside the Cat Senate, the Council was voting for their new leader. This became necessary as Trevenen, who had never given up on finding Maria, had one day left a note for his son that he was going off and was not sure when he might come back—that was six moons past. The Council would have voted sooner but their first choice was reluctant to take the seat of a great leader to whom he would be compared and also reluctant in that this step would signify an admission that Trevenen—his father—would not return.

Huxley, on the previous night sat with Maximus and the Princess, his mate, and they meditated together on the full moon. In the morning Maximus went to the Cat council to announce that Huxley was ready to accept his responsibility if chosen. The two best friends were grown now. Huxley was the wise sage and philosopher, a scholar of the Great Mystery, the ancient texts, and a mystic. He had been groomed to lead by Trevenen, Christopher the Physician, and the presence of Gerald who would appear to him through Stephen the Sparrow, that mischievous yellow dart of a bird that always seemed to know more than his silly nature admitted.

Maximus was now the leader of the Freedom Riders and the bravest of them. He would take any mission, go anywhere, even over the fabled Northwest Passage, often insisting that he go alone and take all the risks on his own. Sometimes he would be gone for many moons, always saying upon his return that he was trying to track down the relentless Reltih whose evil hordes had increased their territory and power. Reltih's influence seemed always to circle ever closer to Catland, encroaching on that sweet place with the negative force of the Second Nature. Only the prevailing Goodness of Catland held off the insidious threat—but for how long.

The goodness of Catland centered on the magic presence of Princess Blue whose love seemed to have no end so that her capacity for giving was equally limitless. She still fascinated her mate, the ever studying, ever contemplating, ever meditating Huxley who worked much harder to understand the Great Mystery intellectually while the Princess seemed to *know* and *be* the Great Mystery intuitively. She was the most selfless creature Catland had ever seen. There was very little *I* in her perception of the world and much more *We*. In that *We* were special places for Huxley, their son Matthias, and Maximus who could not be a more devoted "uncle" just as Matthias could not be a more loving nephew. In a nearby tree Stephen the Sparrow, with the eyes of Gerald, watched Matthias, the boy cat who not only held the rope but also held the future of the world in his little paws.

As Matthias played with his rope, trying to imitate the expert tosses of Maximus, he could hear his hero addressing the Cat Council to nominate Huxley as Council Leader:

"We all miss Trevenen and who could miss him more than Huxley, his son. Yet, we must move forward as I perhaps know better than any of the threats that exist outside this safe haven. In my missions I have seen the influence of the Second Nature in the form of Reltih and his increasing minions outside of Catland. Indeed, it would seem that only here in Catland and to the west in Eagleland that the Second Nature is in no danger of overcoming the First Nature." Maximus paused, thinking of that red-plumed head that he had not seen in the flesh since he carried Wystan back to his home so long before. Of course, in his mind he *saw* and *heard* Wystan always.

"A leader," Maximus continued, "must be a student of history, a believer in the Great Mystery, a scholar of the wise words of Wystan the Wise and Gerald, and he must understand how these truths become a living being to be incorporated in our daily lives. Huxley has devoted his life to this knowledge and the Princess is his great center and guide who keeps his vision focused on love and goodness. Huxley may not have the best eyes, but of us all, he still sees the most. He should be our leader."

In response, Maximus received wholehearted cheers and so it was that Huxley won the vote and took his father's seat as head of the Cat Council. Now a celebration would begin and so would the games and festivities. Maximus, Huxley, and

Princess Blue emerged from the Great Circle where all of Catland waited and applauded. Matthias ran to them, but it was to Maximus first, and the giant said to the boy-cat. "Congratulate your father on this great day."

Matthias then hugged Huxley but soon returned to Maximus. "Show me again Maximus how to loop the rope."

Maximus looked at his best friend and they nodded to each other with understanding. Huxley gave his ascent and Maximus and Matthias went off to the meadow aside the river where all of Catland's children would participate in celebratory games featuring a tug-of-war with the Great Maximus.

As Maximus and Matthias ran off, the Princess took Huxley's paw. "Do not mind him Huxley; he loves you, but often a boy seeks a hero other than his father. And who better than Maximus."

"Yes, who better? Matthias cannot understand his father's need to study the great books and this is not so appealing as compared to the leader of the Freedom Riders and Catland's greatest athlete." Huxley understood this, yet a father always wishes to be a hero to his son.

Princess said, "When he is older and ready for his lessons on the Great Mystery, he will see his father's own greatness—be patient."

"I am."

"I know."

"Still, Princess, sometimes one cannot help but wish one was Maximus."

Princess did not respond, but she knew that it was not so easy to be Maximus, knowing in her heart that at all times Maximus wished he were Huxley. Though never spoken of she knew that Maximus loved her as did Huxley and that when Maximus returned from Eagleland so long ago and found that she had chosen Huxley, the giant cat was far more devastated than she or Huxley could have imagined. Yet Max loved Huxley and would never say a word. Nonetheless, from that time he began going on the most dangerous missions and she had feared he was trying to get killed. In a part of Maximus this was true. Still, in the better part of the giant cat, the part overseen by Wystan and Gerald, Maximus understood that in the plan of the Great Mystery he was supposed to protect all of Catland, especially Huxley, the Princess, and his precious Matthias, who was as close to a son as Maximus would know since he had chosen not to mate.

When Matthias was born, Huxley wished to call him Maximus. Maximus asked that he not do so. Indeed, it was a very rare time as the two almost argued. Princess interceded. She told Huxley that Maximus was afraid for the boy to have his name because he feared what enemies might do. The parents then agreed on the name Matthias, as it was close both to the name Maximus as well as to Huxley's mother's name, Maria. The boy's middle name would be Trevenen.

A Tug of War
• • • • • • • • • • • •

Maximus took his place at one end of the long meadow and hundreds of young cats—many almost young adults—waited at the other end holding one of the long ropes that normally hung on Max's shoulder. Touching the rope was a special thrill for this very rope had accompanied Maximus on his missions, which were legendary and memorized by all of Catland's children. The first young cat in the line was Matthias.

From across the meadow Maximus took the other end of his rope in his giant paws.

The game began: The hundreds of young cats began to pull. Maximus appeared to be almost jerked off his feet but then retained his balance.

They pulled again. Maximus teetered forward but held his place. The crowd cheered.

They pulled harder. He faltered further but then again regained his balance. More cheers.

For a second both sides rested. Maximus appeared to be under great strain and wiped his brow. The children were heartened. (In reality, Maximus was play-acting. Even a thousand could not pull him down.)

They pulled again and Max rolled back and forth—would he fall?

He gave a pull back and straightened himself up. He then looked Matthias straight into his eyes—and Maximus winked, his special signal between himself and Matthias.

The children pulled again and after a few more teeters, Maximus fell forward. The young cats had "won." They cheered but then this roar abated when they saw that Maximus was not moving. They slowly crossed to him. Matthias knelt to sniff the giant cat now lying perfectly still. Then Max leapt to his four paws with a great roar. The children and the citizens of Catland were delighted. Matthias once again hugged his hero. "I knew that no one could really defeat Maximus." Then the boy cat glanced at his father with those strange lunettes that

Christopher the Physician had made just for him—no other cat in Catland needed them.

His father was always reading his books. This did not mean Huxley did not spend time with his son, but such a young boy cat thinks more of outside and games and imagining himself a great warrior rather than a learned scholar. Huxley waved to them both. Matthias nodded back but again turned his face and thoughts to Maximus. The giant black-backed cat observed this perfunctory nod from Matthias to his father and decided it was time for the boy cat to have a lesson. "Come Matthias, walk with me." And they proceeded to the river's edge where the music of the river's flow was always a good setting for learning. They sat on the rock from which Gerald had taught Maximus and Huxley when they were the age Matthias was now.

"Matthias, you know that I love you almost as much as your father and mother do."

"Just 'almost.'"

The giant laughed. "All right, just as much." (And he did.) "And I hope that you love your uncle as well."

"Of course I do."

"Tell me why."

Matthias pondered. "Because you are so big and strong and the bravest cat in Catland."

"And where did my size and strength come from."

Young cats learned early that whatever gifts a creature had came from the Great Mystery and that one should be thankful for these gifts rather than think one was somehow special for having them and deserved more attention because of them.

"I know, from the Great Mystery, but you have also trained to be a warrior and you are the best."

"Perhaps, yet I cannot take any credit that the Great Mystery gave me my size and this size means power—would I be so good a warrior if I were small." Then he paused before saying, "or if I could hardly see."

Matthias understood that Maximus meant his father.

"Years ago, Matthias, when I was determined to rescue Wystan the Wise, only your father would go with me to face who knew what peril. He never hesitated because he was my friend even though he was almost completely blind. And when we were there, he put himself in great danger for my sake and when he had to, he fought well. Now tell me who is braver— the cat whom the Great Mystery has built to be a warrior or a nearly sightless cat who chose to be a warrior despite this disadvantage that he never used as an excuse?"

Matthias looked into his uncle's eyes and understood.

"I neglect him don't I?"

"Yes, your father is the bravest cat I have ever known. Braver than I because he has sacrificed himself to spend countless hours on the Great Learning so he can better bear the responsibility that has now been given him. He will lead all of us and must lead well. What greater courage is there than if one chooses to care for all of Catland and its citizens? It would have been easier for Huxley to use his poor vision as an excuse to say 'let someone else do it.' But he has worked twice as hard because it his destiny."

Matthias hugged Maximus and said. "I know what I must do." And the boy cat went off.

Maximus called after him, "Matthias, there is no need for your father and mother to know of our conversation. Let them believe you have done this on your own."

Matthias found his father in the Meditation Garden with a book. He sat next to him. "What are you reading father?" It was also the destiny of Matthias to become as great a scholar as his father is now.

The Second Nature
•••••••••••••••••

Reltih and Elegnam had just returned from another successful expedition across the wide water to the west and were enjoying their spoils in the coastal stronghold of Nilreb. Reltih's power had grown ever greater and his unofficial army had outposts nearly everywhere in the known world. Only Catland and Eagleland were completely free of Reltih's dangerous ways—for now.

Reltih lit his pipe and then passed it to his second in command. "Tomorrow, Elegnam, it will be ten years."

"I know this well Reltih; you have marked off every day since then in your book."

This was the *Book of the Second Nature* with the rules, lessons, and schemes that would challenge the First Nature. For many generations among the different creatures the First Nature had been the Way and the path to Upward Transcendence embraced by the many to be as normal as breathing. Then humans became more prevalent and the magic language that once was communicated by thought began to be communicated by mouth, and in this spoken and written language something was lost. Each person began to like the sound of his own voice and began to hear it and give it a self-importance that emphasized the *I* instead of the *We*. Each wished to be heard over the others and soon there was competition and then this competition was less about the best and most capable but more about the most powerful and ruthless. In this regard Reltih now had the loudest voice.

Reltih spoke again. "If not for Maximus we would still have Wystan (or so Reltih thought). Slowly we would have broken him and on those special days when the planets would have been in our favor, we would have taken his wisdom of the First Nature and converted that energy to greater power for the Second Nature. We then would be further along in our domination of the world."

"But Reltih, we control most of it and have more than we know what to do with. Is that not a satisfaction?"

"To you perhaps, and that is why you are second and not first in command."

This stung Elegnam who was loyal and nearly as ruthless and cruel as his leader. That was the point—nearly was not good enough for Reltih and instead of respecting Elegnam's many attributes, he mocked him for being second. Reltih could not do otherwise. There was only first, only more, only everything, and there could be no satisfaction in anything less. And while Reltih saw this as the cause of what he supposed was his superiority, this was also his curse. He assumed that if he must be first, then others would wish to replace him. He lived in constant fear and could not sleep for thinking each night that someone was plotting his death. In this he was right. Many wished him dead. But he paid his guards well and made sure they were too dumb to think they could rule an empire themselves. Thus, they believed that they would remain richer in Reltih's service than on their own.

Elegnam said nothing. He was used to these insults, but considered them a small price compared to what he otherwise gained in goods and power. Besides, when stung by Reltih's tongue there were more than enough victims that Elegnam could take his anger out on. He now just listened as Reltih spoke again.

"And if not for Maximus and his Freedom Riders we might even be closer to the territories in and around Catland."

"Yes," Elegnam repeated, "if not for Maximus." To himself Elegnam smiled for he knew how much the Great Cat infuriated Reltih. "And it seems Reltih that since Trevenen gave command of the Riders to Maximus, that Maximus has seen his role in a somewhat different way than Trevenen did. Before Maximus the Riders defended their own and rescued those whom we had taken but that was all—for this was the Code of the Riders, to defend, but not to attack for its own sake."

"Yes, this Maximus thinks he is greater than Trevenen and greater than Huxley. He seeks to not only defend but to go on the offensive with missions to disrupt our operations even though no cats or other creatures need to be protected or rescued."

"We know well Reltih that he uses his claws in a way that Trevenen never would. The soldiers have told me that when Maximus raids the camps his rage is ferocious and there are serious injuries—even fatalities— if anyone attempts to stop him. Just his name strikes fear into our men."

"And what is the cause this rage, Elegnam? He is not like any cat ever before. In Catland anger is a sign of weakness. If

Maximus is angry, what is the weakness or pain that compels him to express this anger? If we knew, we might turn it to our advantage."

Elegnam said, "Our spies believe that perhaps even unknown to himself, he is unconsciously jealous that the Princess chose Huxley over him."

"Yes, Elegnam, the First Nature claims that love is the purpose of life," and Reltih said this with a sneer. "But what of the creature who fails in love? From he pain of this rejection the Second Nature first came into being. Denied earthly love, a creature learns anger. The First Nature asks that creatures be satisfied to love the Great Mystery for itself and that this love is stronger than any other kind so that one should only need this love and not fear losing the love of another. If this were so easy to achieve among our own species, we would not be in power. We give men the goods that they think will make up for not feeling loved. We depend on their selfishness."

"Yet, Reltih, the other creatures seem to accept unselfishness much more easily than humans do."

"Yes, Elegnam, they do don't they, the more fool them— but Maximus with his anger seems to be an exception even if he has no idea that he is. Soon, the planets will be in a favorable alignment again. If we could not have Wystan then perhaps there is another to take the eagle's place—enough of this talk of Maximus. The very thought of him upsets me."

Gerald's Staff

••••••••••••

On the day that Huxley became the leader of the Cat Council he decided to give Gerald's staff to Maximus. Huxley had been concerned over the last year that Maximus was spending more time out of Catland than in Catland. When Huxley would gently inquire of his best friend the nature of these missions, Maximus would just answer that he was "scouting." Yet, Huxley heard the rumors that Maximus was doing more than just scouting. The purpose of giving Maximus the staff was two-fold: The staff should further remind Maximus of Gerald and Gerald's lessons, and, if he was wielding the staff, the staff would not be quite so deadly as those ten long and razor sharp curved hooks that belonged to the warrior cat's giant paws.

Of late, Huxley and the Princess had become more and more worried about Maximus. Moreover, since the day of Huxley's leadership, Matthias spent more time with his father and less with his father's friend. Of this Huxley was pleased and he was sure that Maximus had said something to influence the boy cat. When he would ask Maximus about this, his friend would just say. "Matthias is wise for his age and knows he can learn best from his father the scholar."

And Matthias, as Maximus had asked him to, never revealed their conversation. Indeed, while Huxley was happy to receive more of his son's attention, Maximus found it difficult to have less of it. With the boy, Maximus was better able to soften his heart and hold back the anger that he did not understand. Now, he felt the anger more often and would go on missions more often so that others would not see it. Anger must have an outlet of some kind or it will eat away at the inside.

Cats learn that anger is caused by a creature feeling that he is in some way not in control of his own destiny. This loss of control can derive from many causes. In the outlying territories under Reltih's power, the creatures there had much anger at being under Reltih's thumb. A loss of control can also be felt as a conscious or unconscious desire for something or someone that one cannot have.

Maximus, as brave as he was in the outer world, was no different than anyone else in his inner world, which was not free of troubles. In his mind's confusion there were two questions he often asked himself: "Who am I?" and "What am I to become?"

Huxley and the Princess often talked of their friend.

"Huxley, Maximus becomes more and more distant, more and more silent and withdrawn."

"Yes, I try to speak with him of his introversion and he denies that this is so. Then he changes the conversation. His destiny has not been easy. What is one to think when he was raised under an eagle's wing and has never known who his parents are or anything about his past at all?"

"This is very true, Huxley, and even though I too became an orphan, I knew from whom I came and the history of my tribe."

"Then," Huxley added, "there is also the other matter."

The other 'matter' was themselves, and that the Princess had chosen Huxley.

Ten years before, when Maximus returned from Eagleland, he learned of what had taken place while he was gone—that the inseparable trio could no longer be as they had been when they were children. Maximus took it well then—or seemed to—and the Princess encouraged him to find a mate of his own. He never did. Who could know in these ten years what has gone through his mind? Even Maximus did not understand himself and the cause of his inner anger. Could such a noble soul ever admit that he sometimes had ignoble emotions? It is much easier to deny them and express the anger in another way. This meant his "scouting" missions.

Beasts of Burden
• • • • • • • • • • • • • • •

In one of the territories between Catland and Eagleland there once had roamed freely creatures of the land and air that never took more than they needed. Things changed. A once great elephant was harnessed to a covered wagon containing a heavy load even for him and as he pulled in the summer sun, his once proud head hung low from his captivity and the endless work. Behind him were two horses, once lean stallions with golden hair, fresh and shiny. Now the fur was dirty, matted and dull from their burden of pulling weight for which they were not built to pull. Their heads were even lower. After them were ten of Reltih's hirelings pushing these poor creatures night and day for the sooner they delivered these wagons of stolen goods the sooner they got paid. The pain and suffering of the animals meant nothing to them. And they had long whips for when the creatures seemed too slow. These loads were bound for Nilreb and Reltih himself.

The elephant stopped. The great creature raised his head to look up, the first time in a long time. Of course, when he stopped, the horses also stopped. The men looked ahead and saw the elephant's trunk pointing up. The horses looked where the trunk pointed. Above was a yellow bird fluttering and holding itself in one place just above the elephant's head. The elephant trumpeted and then the horses whinnied.

The men unfurled the long whips and ran ahead to the elephant's rear. They saw the bird hovering and one snapped his whip to try and hit it; the bird was too quick.

The second said, "Forget the stupid bird; we must make the beasts move."

The front two men threw their arms behind their backs preparing to cast their terrible whips forward with vicious snaps. Behind the elephant, the horses, and the men, another pair of eyes saw the poor creatures shake as they braced for the pain that never came. When the men started to bring their arms forward, each arm was suddenly caught and pulled back turning their whole bodies around to learn the cause.

The source was the terror of their bad dreams, the figure that was such a legend that one spoke in whispers of his name and wondered if he was flesh or a demon. None of these men had ever seen him before but there was no mistaking who it was. The wind was billowing the great red cape; the white chest gleamed in the sun; the two long ropes were curled about his shoulders, and the staff of Gerald was bitten between his teeth, revealing fangs that made the humans gasp in fright. The fangs and the face behind them looked very, very angry. The walking nightmare jerked the two whips he held in his paws and the two humans were snapped suddenly to the giant cat's back paws. He reached down and took each by the neck and as he held them off the ground he then splayed his claws to each side of their heads. The other men had no interest in saving anyone but themselves and ran as fast as they could. The two remaining in the great claws were too scared to even beg for their release but closed their eyes and waited for the end to come. And after seeing the cruelty done to the creatures, the causing of their end became for Maximus a terrible temptation.

But then his mind heard the voice of Gerald coming from Stephen the Sparrow. "No, Maximus."

Instead, the men learned that the demon could speak: "Never come this way again; never beat a helpless creature again. I will always know for the yellow sparrow can fly anywhere and he will come and tell me. And then no matter where you go, I will find you."

Then he dropped them to the ground. They too ran and Maximus yelled after them.

"Tell Reltih I will always be here. Tell him he has come far but he will go no further."

Maximus went to the elephant and the two horses. He looked into their eyes and he realized that he had seen them before on the long-ago expedition to free Wystan. Then they had been young, healthy, and free. Now they were so old and beaten he had almost not known them at all.

The elephant's mind spoke. "Do you remember us Maximus?"

"Yes, and of the good company we kept."

The horses said together, "There are many like us, Maximus, and if not for you there would be even more. Without you Reltih would even try to march on Catland and Eagleland. Reltih becomes bolder and bolder because, other than Maximus, no one stands up to him and his army. We fear for the future if he is not stopped."

And the elephant concluded. "Only the great cats are strong enough. Catland cannot isolate itself from the world or soon their isolation will be forced upon them instead of chosen. You must tell them."

As Maximus and the elephant spoke, Stephen was flittering wildly back and forth between the two wagons, sticking his tiny beak here and there in the bales of piled up goods.

Maximus called to him, "Stephen, why are you acting like such a cuckoo bird?"

"He has," the elephant explained, "no doubt found the Amos."

"And what is this Amos?"

"A medicine humans are mad for. It makes them very happy for short periods. And it is very valuable as can be judged by how much effort is taken in transporting and protecting it. Much of the Amos goes to Reltih and he will be very angry when he learns of your visit."

This thought aroused Max's curiosity. "Do you think he will come for his Amos?"

"I am sure of it. The crystals form on the Amos plant only in the spring and this is the last of it until next spring." Then Maximus freed the creatures from their harnesses and they said their farewells. They did not know that they would see each other again soon.

Reltih Rides

• • • • • • • • • • •

Four of the ten men returned to Nilreb—six were afraid to face Reltih and fled to take their chances living in the wilderness. These remaining four had the special knowledge of where the Amos plants were and how to harvest the crystals so knew they would be spared. The other six had no such bargaining position. Reltih was furious, stamping and sputtering until he was red in the face

He said over and over, "Will not someone rid me of this cat?" He looked about him and did not see any volunteers. "What good are any of you?" He pulled his sword and moved towards them but Elegnam stopped him, whispering to Reltih "We need them."

Instead Reltih ordered that his best guards immediately prepare to retrieve the Amos now sitting somewhere in the sun. To the four he ordered that they lead the guards to the cargo. Then to his servant, "Prepare my elephant, I will go with them."

The expedition came upon the covered wagons the next morning. The beasts of burden were gone, and since the wagons were in the open, Reltih and his guards could see nothing else around and they proceeded to retrieve their precious goods. The cargo still seemed to be inside and with the coverings over it the Amos probably had not yet been damaged by the wind and sun.

Reltih whipped his elephant until the creature winced in pain and then rode quickly to his valuable cargo as the guards tried to keep up with their anxious master. Reltih reached the first wagon, dismounted, pulled aside the high cover, and received the shock of his life. From behind him all the guards could see was that Reltih was suddenly snapped upward and he appeared to be dangling in the air, his legs twitching madly. In fact, he was in the grasp of Max's left paw.

His throat squeezed, he creaked out, "attack him!" The guards, though terrified, ran to the wagon. One guard jumped up to it. Maximus raised his giant paw and splayed his terrible claws. The guard's eyes were wide with the idea that his time was at hand. Max, however, listening to his better part, retracted the claws and merely swatted the guard as one would a fly. More guards came forward. Maximus took Gerald's staff from between his teeth and its seven-foot length swept the knees of these unfortunates and they crumbled rearward to the earth.

Maximus told Reltih, "Stop them or I will finish crushing your neck."

Reltih croaked, "Stop!"

The guards were very willing to obey.

Reltih had never seen Maximus and until now had disbelieved the stories of his size and strength; indeed, he now considered them underestimates. Maximus uncoiled a section of one of his long ropes, retaining the rest, and tied the loose end around Reltih's waist, dropping him in a lump back to the ground but on a short leash.

Maximus said, "Keep your guards at bay or I will snap you back up just as fast." Reltih put his hand up for his men to obey. This was hardly necessary. None wanted any part of Maximus. "Now Reltih, you and I must talk."

From the ground as if to a great height Reltih shouted, "How do you know if I am he?" Maximus knew because his faithful scout Stephen had told him so but merely answered. "I know much more than you can imagine."

Reltih didn't try to deny it. "So, at last, the two most powerful creatures in the world meet."

Maximus smiled to himself thinking that if Reltih couldn't kill him he would try to flatter him. He did not reply and let Reltih stew in his own fear for a moment. Then Reltih tried bribery. "Maximus, why should we feud? Imagine what we could do together instead of being enemies."

This approach was as feeble as the flattery. If Maximus wished to follow his Second Nature and do evil instead of good, he would not need anyone's help to do so. He still did not speak although he did jerk Reltih on his rope to show him that at the moment only one of them was really the most powerful.

Then Maximus asked, "How do you like being harnessed and harassed as your guards have done to so many of the Great Mystery's beautiful creatures?

Reltih wished it were Maximus who was leashed. What a prize and what a price the giant cat would bring if he could ever be captured.

"What do you want Maximus?

"I want for you to know that your expansion will go no further. The peaceful nations have given in to your lies about treaties in order to appease you and prevent violence. But then you do violence anyway. I will not appease you Reltih. I wish it were not so that you have as much as you have already conquered but now you are too close to Catland and Eagleland. You will stop or I will stop you."

"You are only one Maximus." When Reltih said it his guards thought that in the case of Maximus one was more than enough. "And you cannot be everywhere."

"Perhaps I will not always be able to prevent your tyranny when it happens, but know well that when I find out, I can undo whatever you have done. The more you try to go against my will, the angrier I will become." Maximus again splayed his claws and showed his great fangs.

The humans, including Reltih, cowered and then their leader spoke again. "You mentioned the Great Mystery, which your fellow cats believe in so fervently. If you are one of them, then you cannot kill except in self-defense. The Great Cat Council forbids it."

"The Council has never known one such as you. They do not understand such greed and your terrible yearning for power that is the goal in itself. Cats do not seek power for its own sake so they cannot recognize how much of a threat that you are."

"I am merely a businessman who trades well."

"Or steals well is what you should say."

"Maximus, one hears that the Cat Council is disturbed by your expeditions."

Maximus did not answer.

"And if the Council tells you to stop, you must stop or be ostracized from Catland."

Maximus knew this was true, but if he stopped, soon there might not be a Catland.

As he thought this he slowly reeled in Reltih and pulled him back up to eye level, which meant that Reltih was once more swinging like a puppet. Maximus had him now and could end all of Reltih's terror in an instant. The urge to do so was enormous. Maximus clenched and unclenched his claws over and over.

He couldn't do it. Maximus untied the rope from Reltih's waist and dropped him to the ground again.

"Be gone with you and your guards Reltih. And remember what I have told you. Remember also that I spared you."

Oh, yes, Reltih would remember but not with kindness. Reltih considered it as weakness and was already plotting his revenge. His men picked him up and they set off to return to Nilreb. Reltih considered asking Maximus if he could take the Amos but then thought better of it. The thought of being without it just made him angrier.

Conflict in Catland
• • • • • • • • • • • • • • • • • •

When Maximus and Stephen returned to Catland a few days later, Maximus received a message that there was to be a meeting of the Cat Council the next morning. That night he saw Huxley, Princess, and Matthias. They sat in the meditation garden together. Huxley did not ask Maximus about his most recent expedition. Maximus was not too surprised as he would always just answer "scouting" and he assumed Huxley felt no need to hear the same answer again. Maximus knew if he told his friend the truth that Huxley would keep their trust as his friend, but if he told Huxley the leader of the Cat Council the truth, then Huxley could not keep it from the Council.

Maximus wished to change the subject and asked Matthias if he was progressing in his lessons.

"Most certainly," the boy cat answered. "Is this not so father?"

"Indeed, Maximus, I believe he is further along than I was at his age."

Maximus teased, "that's not saying much," but he gave that special wink to Matthias as he said it. Huxley laughed and was glad his good friend could still make a joke and not be so serious all the time. The Princess agreed, saying, "It is nice to see you smile Maximus. This reminds me of when we were three silly kittens playing by the river."

"Yes," Huxley agreed, "those were good times." The Princess said, "Come, Matthias, it is time for you to go to sleep." The boy cat was reluctant to leave Maximus whom he saw much too little of these days with his constant expeditions. He gave in after Maximus promised to play with him the next morning.

Then Huxley said, "And speaking of tomorrow, Maximus, there is something I must tell you."

Huxley's tone was serious. "The Cat Council has pressed me for this meeting. They wish to question you."

"About what?" Although Maximus was sure he already knew.

"Your expeditions."

"Cannot they let sleeping cats lie?"

"I wish they could—tell me Maximus, is there anything you wish me to know."

"Many things, but as your friend, I will not put you in the position of having to choose between me and the Cat Council. If you do not know, you cannot lie."

"But . . ."

"Good night, Huxley. Know always that I love you like a brother and so too love the Princess and Matthias." Maximus abruptly left without another word.

In the early morning, Maximus showed Matthias some new rope tricks in the long meadow by the river where Matthias reminded him of the tug-of-war. It was good to laugh together for who knew what today would bring, and when they would see each other again. The boy cat was as if his own son, especially as Maximus knew it would not be his destiny to mate.

Huxley came to them. "It is time for the meeting, Maximus."

All of the Council members were present and there were many citizens of Catland in the surrounding gallery. Apparently, the meeting was of some importance. Huxley took the leader's chair just as his father had done for so long. There had been no word from Trevenen, and Huxley missed him very much. The new leader called for order then asked the Cat Secretary to announce the first item on the Agenda.

The secretary rose and read. "The Council wishes Maximus to stand in the witness box and account for his actions away from Catland over the last two moons."

Maximus went to the box that was next to Huxley, and he could barely squeeze into it. The box had been built for normal-sized cats.

Senator Leopardus stood to ask the questions. Leopardus had been much disappointed when Huxley was chosen over him.

"Maximus," he asked, "can you describe to us the general nature of your most recent expeditions?"

"Scouting."

"To see what?"

"To see that no enemies were near Catland."

"Did you succeed in this?"

"Apparently, as I have heard no reports that Catland was attacked while I was gone."

This jest elicited laughter from the gallery until Huxley called for silence.

"I am glad," Leopardus rejoined, "to see that you return to us in a good humor." He paused and then posed his next question. "Did you see any creatures at all?"

"Many—elephants, horses, bears, apes, birds, particularly Stephen the Sparrow who faithfully traveled with me everywhere to keep a promise he made long ago to watch over me."

A friendly voice from the gallery yelled, "And no doubt, our brave friend, it is now you who watches over the sparrow just as you watch over all of Catland." The gallery cheered. It was clear on whose side their sentiments belonged. Huxley again called for silence, saying he would empty the gallery for a closed session if there were further interruptions.

Leopardus played the diplomat. "Of course, Maximus, all of Catland respects your efforts to defend our way of life. Yet, one can consider if that in one's efforts to protect a way of life, one bends the rules of that way of life."

Maximus was not inclined to be so diplomatic. "Be bold Leopardus and make plain what you wish to say."

"Did you see humans?"

"Perhaps."

"Did you attack humans?"

"I have been given the mandate by this very Council to protect Catland."

"Yes, Maximus, to *defend* Catland from *attack* or to retrieve kidnapped cats or stolen goods."

"Yes."

"This Council questions if you have acted only in self-defense."

"That will depend on how one defines what is meant 'attack.'"

"Come now, Maximus, can we all agree that to attack means if a creature besets you with intent to harm?"

"How so harm—with a blow by a club, with a cut from a blade? Yes these are obvious attacks. Yet, there are more subtle ways to attack. There is the deliberate work to overcome all of a country's neighbors so that the enemy surrounds the country. There is a conspiracy to cut off trade or raise prices in these neighboring countries that are controlled by these very enemies who have subjugated our neighbors because we would not help our neighbors. And then by damaging the country's economy, the enemy will make this country more vulnerable in the near future. These are attacks that are just the same as, and can be even more effective than the club or sword."

Indeed, Leopardus knew that much of this was true but one hopes it will stop. "But if Reltih is ignored and especially not provoked, surely he would leave Catland alone." The goal of those who agreed with Leopardus was that Reltih should not in any way be provoked. "Maximus, we understand that you mistrust Reltih but so far he has done nothing to us directly."

Maximus did not agree. "Do you forget how the Princess came to be here—all of her tribe suddenly disappeared. Or how I came to be here—rescued from the terrible cave. And how I freed Wystan the Wise." (He didn't bother to add that Wystan could have freed himself.)

"That was long ago."

"Does that mean you believe Reltih has changed."

Leopardus paused for a moment then continued, "We believe that perhaps it is you that has changed Maximus."

"If I am fulfilling my duty to protect Catland, then I am the same Maximus."

"Is there not a difference in protecting by defending rather than going on the offensive, which is forbidden by the *Book of the Cat Council?*"

Maximus was sorely tempted to give details of his recent encounter with Reltih but in words alone he knew he could not convey the images of the enslaved elephant and horses that symbolized the more pervasive tyranny that now surrounded Catland. Instead, he said, "Does it not say also in the Book that we are to protect and defend those who are in danger?"

"Yes, *cats* that are in danger."

Huxley the scholar interrupted to say, "No Leopardus, the Book never says only cats."

"But it was written by cats."

"Yes," Huxley answered, "long before we were born. Who is to say now that they only meant cats or all of the creatures put here by the Great Mystery?"

"Perhaps, Huxley, yet we can never know for sure can we?"

"I cannot imagine," Huxley countered, "that the ancient sages would have been so narrow as to not extend their love and good will to all living creatures rather than just themselves."

Then he asked of Maximus, "Maximus, have you protected and defended creatures that needed such help?"

"Yes."

"For themselves alone?"

"For them and for Catland as well. Someday it will be said, 'that which is done to the least of them is done to me.' If we ignore the suffering of others, then our turn will come and there will be no one left to help us because we didn't help others when we should have. It is not enough to say that we must isolate ourselves if we are not directly attacked. This systematic subjugation of the surrounding territories is not going to stop until it reaches our border and then it may be too late for us. If this is not a threat to Catland, we are all mistaken."

As Maximus said this, Leopardus signaled to an aide. The aide brought forth a human whose face was covered by a mask. Leopardus said of this human, "We have a witness who says that Maximus has gone too far." Leopardus pushed the man forward. "Speak!"

The human was nervous. He looked like a traveling trader. He said, "I was carrying a cargo bound for Nilreb when the giant cat appeared. He attacked and beat the elephant and two horses that pulled our wagons and then chased the humans away. After which from behind trees we watched him destroy our goods and finish the elephant and horses."

Maximus shouted, "This is an outrageous lie!"

Huxley spoke, "Impossible, Maximus would never hurt defenseless creatures. I have seen the opposite for years."

Leopardus asked the human, "Do you stand by your account?"

"Yes. And I must tell you that many live in fear of the giant cat and one hears that this instance is not the only one."

Maximus shouted again, "Do you not see he has been paid to lie? Do you not see that this is more of Reltih's propaganda just as he has used propaganda so well in his expansion?"

The man shook his head. "I tell the truth."

Maximus protested, "If he is a truth-teller, why must he hide his face."

Leopardus signaled for the human to be taken away and then said, "Because he is afraid of reprisal from you, Maximus."

The entire gallery was stunned into silence. Maximus understood what game was being played but was too proud to say any more. If after more than ten years in Catland, his character was not known, what else could he possibly say?

Huxley stood up from the chair that had once been Trevenen's. "I speak now not as leader of the Council but as a friend to Maximus. I am glad my father is not here to see this. He regarded Maximus as a second son and raised him to love and to serve. I do not believe Maximus would do such things and we would be foolish to imagine that it is not possible for a plot of words to be made against him. Maximus makes much sense. The world has changed; we cannot ignore these changes and pretend that they may not affect us. Yes, it is easier to look the other way, but is it wise?" Huxley sat again indicating he had now resumed his role as leader.

Leopardus called for a vote as to whether Maximus should continue as the principal defender of Catland. He also asked for the gallery to be cleared before the vote.

Huxley protested, as there had never been a closed vote before. He realized that already Reltih was affecting the ways of Catland. Huxley demanded a vote to decide if the vote should be closed. The closed vote won. The citizens in the Gallery were removed but not without many shouts of protest.

The Council proceeded to the vote on Maximus. The tally was close, but fear overruled good sense. Maximus was removed as the Captain of the Freedom Riders.

The giant cat that had devoted himself to Catland now walked out, ignoring even the pleas of Huxley to stay. The citizens had waited outside and could tell by Max's grim face the result. He walked through them without a word though they made it clear they wished him to stay. Huxley followed his friend who was stepping faster and faster in the direction of the river and to the bridge out of Catland. When Maximus reached the water's edge, Matthias was there playing with the rope his uncle had made for him. Matthias saw the giant cat and the crowd behind him with his father shouting, "Maximus, wait!" Matthias ran up to Maximus. "What has happened? What is wrong?"

The great warrior cat stopped for only a moment and dropped to one knee to look into the face of this beloved boy cat. "Know you, Matthias, that I will always love all of Catland, especially your mother and father, but most of all I will miss you." He then stood up, crossed the bridge, and on all fours ran off at a speed no other cat could possibly match, determined never to return.

That night, Huxley felt a grief he had not known since finding Trevenen's mysterious note. Now both of his heroes were gone. He wanted to resign as leader of the Council. The

Princess knew better. "No, Huxley, then Leopardus will have more influence and his policies of appeasement to Reltih will be even more pronounced. Maximus would not want this."

At the sound of his best friend's name, Huxley took off his lunettes and buried his nearly sightless eyes into his mate's gray chest. At this moment, the scholar cat that had studied so much and long so that his mind might see what his eyes could not, wished to see nothing at all, so large was the pain in his heart.

Matthias had never seen his father like this. He hoped he never would again. The boy cat understood how his father felt for he also felt a great sadness that the giant shadow of Maximus might never again appear before the entrance of their burrow to signal his coming.

The boy cat took his rope and hugged it until he fell asleep. The Princess, no less than they, could not imagine life without Maximus. For when that time had come long ago for her to choose, it had been with the greatest difficulty, as she had loved them both. The decision came from her great instinct to give of herself to the one she believed needed her most. And this seemed to be the sightless Huxley. Who now could say, if in his own way, Maximus, the orphan without a past, was even more in need of her comfort? While all three were sad, Huxley and Matthias did not also have the additional burden that the Princess carried. For in her deepest heart she knew that Maximus would never have left Catland if she were his mate. This knowledge was heavy on her. Only the Great Mystery could know why such a destiny was necessary. She wished so much that Gerald could be here.

A moment later Stephen the Sparrow flew in and alighted on her shoulder. Now she could sleep.

By morning the sparrow was gone. He had flown off to catch up with Maximus. It did not matter that he did not know which way Max had gone. The sparrow closed his eyes and let the Great Mystery navigate for him.

A Year later:
• • • • • • • • • • •

Huxley was in the watchtower he had built shortly after Maximus left Catland. He built it so that he might see his friend return. His sight was limited, but he would know Maximus if he saw him. He had not seen him yet.

Matthias called from below, "Come down, father; it is time to eat." In truth, Princess had sent their son to fetch Huxley as he had been in his tower most of the day as he was nearly every day. After Maximus left, Huxley took up the giant cat's cause. He urged the Cat Council to heed Max's warnings of Reltih's treachery. Without the backing of Maximus, Huxley had less authority and Leopardus more. In two moons after Max's exit, the Council called for a new election and Leopardus narrowly won, replacing Huxley as leader. Hence, Huxley had more time on his paws to build the tree tower and stand upon it with his head turning his eyes in all directions.

Although he had not seen Maximus, Huxley, as did all of Catland, had heard many stories about his adventures. One faction of Catland thought Max a hero as he continued his excursions against Reltih. The other faction thought him a criminal. Meanwhile Reltih's sphere of influence was edging ever closer to Catland. The more Leopardus gave in to Reltih's will, the more Reltih exerted his will. The squeeze was on. Appeasement was not working, just as Maximus had predicted.

While Maximus was not seen, he was heard of as there was a steady flow of stories coming from travelers and traders: "The midnight ghost raided a caravan and freed all of the harnessed animals," or "The Great Maximus boldly stormed an Outlaw city in the middle of the day to prevent scheduled executions of so-called traitors against Reltih," or "Maximus canceled the delivery of weapons to territorial forces by waiting for the wagons to traverse a mountain pass and then pushing them off the mountain."

The supporters of Maximus cheered at the reports of these exploits. Those opposed believed that Maximus was just inciting a potential war with Reltih's ever-growing forces against Catland. The latter were mistaken. Reltih was crazy for power but not stupid. The cats, if attacked, would be the most dangerous army on earth. Even a victory would be so costly as to be madness. Reltih's plan was to isolate Catland and choke it off from the outside world, leaving him in total control. No, Reltih would wait. The longer the cats appeased him, the more difficult it would be for them to wake up and resist. Catland would be a land-locked island cut off to slowly starve itself out of existence.

Each day, Huxley mounted his watchtower and asked the Great Mystery for the return of Maximus. He had considered going off to join his friend, but he could not bring himself to leave the Princess and Matthias. In recent days some of the members of the Cat Council had mysteriously disappeared. The link between these missing cats was their vocal opposition to Reltih. The tyrant was becoming bolder. Huxley was not afraid for himself but for his mate and son if he was not there to protect them. Meanwhile in Nilreb, Reltih cursed the midnight ghost who was becoming more than just a nuisance.

The Rebel Resistors
••••••••••••••••••

Maximus was encouraging the seeds of resistance to grow in the territories. Now there was an underground movement of Freedom Fighters that were also disrupting Reltih's march to total power.

A messenger slinked into Reltih's quarters with a message. He knew the content and wanted to get out before the master read it. He handed the note over and turned quickly to leave. No such luck.

"Wait!" Reltih ordered, "to see if this message needs a reply."

The message was from Elegnam who was out in the territories leading a caravan.

We reached the ocean and waited for the ships to take our cargo across. Maximus and a herd of free elephants charged. Our forces fled at the sight of such a rush of giants. Then the raiders pushed the Amos into the ocean, destroying it. The ships soon arrived but we had nothing to give them. The captain of the fleet was furious. He wanted to know if Reltih would pay for the expense of the wasted trip. Since he represents our principle buyer, I agreed, as I feared that if he left without this agreement, we would lose their business.

Reltih roared and ripped the message to pieces. The messenger shook. Reltih gave him a note for Elegnam that read, "Return immediately. We must act and stop Maximus now before he inspires a total rebellion."

When Elegnam arrived, he needed to give Reltih much of his Amos to reduce his ranting and raving to a mere seething anger so they could scheme.

Reltih spit out, "We must hunt him down, corner him and take him into the captivity. This would demoralize his supporters more than if we merely killed him. Then Maximus would be the hero martyr and they might still be inspired to resist."

"We have tried, Reltih, but he is too smart and too fast. We can never catch up to him; it seems he has eyes that can see us long before we arrive and can corner him."

These were Stephen's eyes. They knew nothing of the sparrow for who could have thought that a tiny bird was the great ally to Maximus.

Elegnam said, "I know, Reltih, another way to flush him out."

Yes, for the past year Stephen the Sparrow was Max's ally and closest friend to whom the giant cat spoke to of his inner heart. Maximus missed Catland dearly and Stephen encouraged him to return.

"No Stephen, if I return I might find it impossible to tear myself away again and continue our work, and I also fear that if I return, I will just put Catland in danger."

Stephen knew Maximus was right but the sparrow also knew that the giant cat's heart was broken.

More and more Maximus missed Catland and more and more his sadness darkened his heart and turned to anger. His raids became more frequent, his attacks more ferocious. The anger seethed and soon resentment grew in the giant cat's mind. If one feels anger, one cannot help but need someone to blame for feeling this anger. At first Maximus blamed Reltih, but over time, he began to find fault with Catland itself. Anger can play tricks on the mind and Max's mind was becoming bitter at what he considered his ostracism from Catland. In his self-imagined exile, he even began to give part of the blame to Huxley for not defending him more. This, of course, was not the case. Indeed, the mind does play tricks.

Stephen saw these changes in Maximus and again urged the giant cat to at least make brief visits to Catland and leave again before Reltih could do anything about it. Max wouldn't even discuss it and made the sparrow promise not to go to Catland on his own. Max did not want Huxley or anyone else to look for him. Thus, Maximus remained a cat alone. Yes, he did have the company of Stephen and the other creatures, but a cat misses cats.

In Nilreb, Reltih became increasingly agitated and infuriated at Max's activities. Max's resistance forces were growing larger and even some humans joined. Reltih now could not sleep at all and this could not go on. His empire was being seriously threatened.

Matthias

·········

The Princess had just finished her regular visit to Catland's senior citizen burrow where she had brought food and good cheer and helped the old cats with chores and errands. She went to see the kitten kindergarten and read to them from the *Book of Cat Fables.* Even these little ones wanted her to talk of the great Maximus and she told them stories of when she and Huxley and Maximus were kittens. The kitten kindergarten was located on the way to the long meadow by the river. After leaving the adorable kittens Princess walked there to meet Matthias who was still mastering the rope Maximus gave him. She did not see him there. She assumed Matthias returned home or went with Huxley for a walk in the Meditation Gardens.

Their burrow was empty. Princess went to the Gardens. They were not there. She returned to the burrow and saw Huxley. She asked, "Have you seen Matthias?"

"No, I thought he was with you."

Both looked in the places that Matthias might have gone. They asked his friends if they'd seen him. They hadn't. Huxley and Princess mounted the watchtower. From it one could see very far, but they could not see far enough to locate Matthias.

They made haste to the bridge that crossed the river. At the bridge was the Horn of Welcome that could also be the Horn of Warning if necessary. Huxley sounded the horn and in moments all the citizens of Catland were at the bridge.

Huxley told them, "We cannot find Matthias." The cats fanned out and searched everywhere until the sunset and a moonless night came interrupting the search. Huxley and the

Princess stayed awake all night waiting for any sign. They were both frightened and the Princess was beside herself with distress.

The next morning the search began anew now to include the near territories outside of Catland. Nothing. And this was very strange as there were no tracks or scent at all. If Matthias had wandered away on his own, there would be a trail.

By dusk all of the cats returned to Catland without a clue.

A grim reality beset Huxley and the Princess. Matthias was kitnapped.

The Princess collapsed from grief and Huxley carried her to their burrow.

A mother's instinct is strong. The Princess knew what this was about.

At that moment Christopher the Physician ran in. His face was alarmed.

"I have just received a message." He gave it to Huxley and Princess. The note had no signature. It didn't need one.

"We have the boy cat at the horseshoe plateau. Tell Maximus."

Huxley roared and the Princess hugged him.

She asked him, "What can we do?"

"This is a plan to stop Maximus."

Princess, the mother, could not help but put Matthias first. "Maximus loves Matthias. He will help."

Huxley hesitated, "But surely this is a trap and there are no guarantees for either Maximus or Matthias." For once the great scholar was uncertain. "I don't know what to do."

She did. The Princess closed her eyes and thought of Gerald.

Stephen the Sparrow was flying about and scouting for Max's resistance forces. In mid-flight, he suddenly stopped and fluttered his tiny wings in place hovering in one spot. His eyes were closed for a moment. Then they opened and he darted at his greatest speed back to Maximus.

The giant cat was sleeping with his back against a tree. He had just returned with four elephants from one of Reltih's forts near the wide water. The fort was no longer standing. Maximus was exhausted. His missions were consuming him, and he rarely slept through a whole night. This lack of sleep further fanned his anger and resentment. Bitterness was creeping into his mind. He began to wonder if enough was enough. If Catland didn't appreciate him, why should he go on? These thoughts came from his Second Nature, which was challenging his First Nature for dominance over Max's mind. One does not even want to imagine what might happen if his Second Nature won.

Stephen flew into the camp and fluttered in place in front of Max's closed eyes until they opened. "Maximus, I have a message from Catland."

There had been many previous messages but Maximus had refused to hear them.

Now was no different. "What is that to me?" His present state of mind wanted no news of Catland. This would just make him angrier.

"But Maximus—"

Maximus stood up and walked away from Stephen. The elephants and other creatures watched the scene with puzzlement; as of late they were concerned with the mental state of their leader.

The sparrow flew after him, circling the great head. Maximus waved his paw to bid Stephen desist.

"But, Maximus—"

The paw jerked again and struck Stephen, stunning the little bird that then fell to the ground. The creatures were shocked. Maximus stopped. He could not believe what he had just done. He put both paws to his head and shook himself as if to shake out his temporary madness. His First Nature defeated his Second Nature. Maximus reached down and cupped the little sparrow in his two paws, lifting him up to his face. "I am sorry and ashamed my old friend. Will you forgive me?"

The sparrow flew to Max's right shoulder and in Stephen's voice said, "Nothing to forgive." Then the tiny bird flew to the left shoulder and in the voice of Gerald asked, "Will you now hear the message from Catland?"

"Yes, and any more that follow this one. My anger is gone."

"Then the First Nature is again your only Nature."

"Yes! What is the message?"

The sparrow thought how the anger that just had left Maximus was going to return very quickly. Then he told him: "Reltih has taken Matthias to the Horseshoe Plateau." The giant cat spread his arms and roared with such force that the other creatures covered their ears.

From the watchtower Huxley and the Princess looked over the far plains and the even further mountains. They thought they heard distant thunder but as the echo crossed the great distance they knew better. Huxley put his paw around the princess and said, "It is Maximus."

The echo carried over their heads and to all corners of Catland. Cats stopped their work, emerged from their burrows, and then began walking to the watchtower by the bridge. They gathered until all of Catland was present. Christopher the Physician called up to Huxley, "Is that our friend, we hear." Huxley nodded yes. The citizens cheered.

Leopardus climbed the tower. Huxley braced for a conflict. The Cat Council Leader reached the top. Instead of conflict, Leopardus embraced Huxley, saying to him, "I was wrong and Maximus was right. Will you tell him that when you see him?" Then Leopardus turned to the gathered cats. He raised Huxley's paw with his own, and said. "Now is the time for all good cats to stand together against our enemy Reltih. And now is the time to follow one leader and that is Huxley." The cats cheered again. Huxley and Leopardus embraced a second time and Huxley thanked his former rival.

Above their heads a yellow dart had witnessed all. Stephen flew down to Princess Blue's shoulder. He said to her in Gerald's voice, "I heard you." And then to Huxley in Stephen's giggly voice, "It's about time you and Maximus stopped being silly. Maximus will meet you at his camp in the mountains to the east of Nilreb. I will lead you there and any cats may join you that wish to do so."

Huxley called down to the cats. "Maximus waits for us. Who will join me?"

Leopardus spoke first. "I will."

Then the Freedom Riders stepped forward. "We will go to be with our Captain again."

Christopher stepped forward. Then all of Catland followed Christopher.

Huxley and the Princess waved their thanks. Then Huxley said, "We cannot all go. Many must remain to look after Catland?"

It was decided that Huxley, Leopardus, and the Freedom Riders would go to signify that Catland was now united against Reltih.

The Princess said goodbye to her mate. "Be careful, Huxley. Tell Maximus I miss him. Bring back Matthias." She hesitated, and then said, "Bring him back one way or another." She meant alive or dead but could not bring herself to say these words. Stephen the Sparrow led the rescuers out of Catland to join Maximus and his resistance force.

A Reunion
• • • • • • • • • •

"It is good to see you again my old friend," Huxley said to Maximus.

"I have missed all of you more than I can say and for a long time more than I realized."

"We are together now and that is all that matters."

"And of our little boy cat I have good news. Stephen has seen Matthias in the horseshoe plateau and he is alive."

"Thank goodness."

"The sparrow has flown to tell the Princess and will return soon."

That night Maximus, Huxley, Leopardus, and the Freedom Riders planned and plotted the rescue of Matthias. Many suggestions were made; many were ultimately rejected. No plan would be easy or without the greatest danger to themselves and to Matthias. Maximus listened. He was thinking that after Stephen saw the Princess, the sparrow would fly to the horseshoe plateau for one more look at the stronghold and return with his report.

Stephen was high overhead of Reltih's fortress. He flew in undetected circles, noting the number of men, where they were deployed, and most importantly that Matthias was still well. This was easy because unlike previous captives, Matthias was not in the terrible cave. He was out in the open, tied by a short rope to a small tree. As he was making his last circle, Stephen saw Reltih far below. The sparrow descended a bit closer and fluttered in place just over Reltih's black-haired head. Reltih was speaking to Elegnam when suddenly he felt something splat on the top of his head and cursed terribly while looking up for the culprit. The sparrow's aim had been true and Stephen flew out of the horseshoe plateau giggling with great satisfaction.

Maximus and his fellows retired for the evening although none would sleep well as they prepared for the daring mission they would undertake. The giant cat had said little during the meeting nor listened particularly well because he had made his own plan.

He understood that the purpose of Reltih's abduction of Matthias was to make the boy cat bait for getting Maximus. If Reltih saw any of the other would-be rescuers, he might kill the boy cat immediately. It was Maximus that Reltih wanted, and Maximus that Reltih would get one way or another. The warrior cat knew that if he was unable to rescue Matthias he would offer himself in exchange for Matthias. Huxley and the others might try to prevent him and who knew what Reltih would do. Yes, long before Huxley and the others would be aware of it, Maximus would already be on his way to the horseshoe plateau.

At dawn the Princess climbed the watchtower and waited. Below the citizens of Catland waited with her.

Reltih and Elegnam also climbed a watchtower overlooking the narrow width of the entrance to the plateau. On the top edges of the plateau to each side of the opening were the scaffolds upon which were piled the giant rocks that were meant to be thrown down at approaching enemies. The evil duo looked out into the far plain but as yet saw nothing.

Reltih was highly agitated, nearly frantic with anxiety. Would Maximus come?

"Where is he, Elegnam? Perhaps he is not so brave after all."

"He will come. One way or another he will show himself."

Reltih turned around in a complete circle to look at his stronghold. "Is everything ready?"

For at least the tenth time since sunrise, Elegnam answered, "Yes, Master, Everything is ready."

"There is no way he can possibly sneak in."

"Only if he can fly."

Reltih put his hand to his ear and leaned outward over the opening. "I thought I heard something."

Elegnam likewise curved his ear. "A slight rumbling, perhaps, is it distant thunder?"

Slowly, the rumbling grew louder if not yet loud but it was a steady drone, not the sporadic claps that thunder makes.

Reltih said, "It sounds like a beast running. Could it be him?" They both peered out and as the rumbling increased in volume, they began to see the wisp of a cloud far off.

Elegnam wondered aloud, "Is that dust?"

The wisp, as did the sound, also grew and seemed like a moving cloud of flying dirt. And that cloud was moving straight for them.

Reltih yelled to his attendant, "Blow the horn," and a coarse signal sounded throughout the horseshoe plateau. Reltih's hordes, already alert, doubled their attention as they too could begin to hear that rumbling getting closer and closer.

The dust cloud was also nearer, its hazy tan color starkly clear against the darker plain and blue sky.

"Elegnam, is it Maximus? Would he come in broad daylight?"

"Perhaps he thought we'd be more prepared for him at night and he hopes to take us by surprise."

"Well," Reltih said, "the stupid fool does not know how much noise he makes and the dust that he stirs up. We are ready aren't we?"

To brace for this frontal assault, Elegnam waved forward the greater number of Reltih's hordes to place themselves at the narrow opening. They were to stand just out of sight. It would not do for Maximus to see them and change his mind. No, Maximus must enter the opening so he could be trapped within. Then Reltih would have both Maximus and the son of Huxley together. The soldiers were armed with swords and better yet arrows and spears that could wound the giant cat without their getting too close to his deadly claws. At the top of the plateau over the entrance were two soldiers next to the rock-bearing scaffolds. They were waiting to throw down the largest stones that could knock Maximus to the ground.

The rumbling was now shaking the earth with the force of the giant cat's incredible speed. The cloud of dust was darker and thicker so that nothing could be seen within it. This cloud's movement was quick and steady. The sound of the pounding steps was now as loud as the thunder they first thought it might be, but a thunder as if directly overhead. The men by the scaffolds covered their ears while they tried to keep their balance, as it seemed the earth was trembling and making them perform a terrible dance. The hordes were becoming fearful. To almost all of them the Great Maximus was a frightening legend but one they had not yet seen. And those few who had seen him made him sound just as fearsome as the others could have possibly imagined. Now here was this giant monster advancing so powerfully that he shook the very earth under their feet.

With all the eyes fixed on the moving cloud, no one noticed the yellow dart above them who was there to give signals that required the most perfect timing. Yes, Maximus was running at an incredible speed and the sound of his steps needed to cease with the utmost precision. To this need, Stephen the Sparrow was giving his greatest attention. The yellow dart suddenly flew straight up, and as he did the cloud slowed and the thunder of the steps lessened until both the cloud and the steps came to a halt, just short of the narrow opening.

Reltih yelled, "What is he doing?"

No one could answer. But all of Reltih's forces had been drawn to the sight and sound of the cloud and were now massed at the entrance of the horseshoe plateau. Maximus had, indeed, stopped running so that the sound of his steps would not give his position away.

Hundreds of anxious eyes stared at the cloud that was now gradually clearing with a slowness that was torture. All were waiting to see the giant cat Maximus. Every head edged closer to get a better view. They saw a shape—wait, not just one—was Maximus not alone?

The dust dissipated and revealed—not Maximus—but elephants, a hundred of them. Every pair of eyes was wide and all seemed hypnotized by the sight. Where was Maximus?

From behind them, after his running start, the sound of which was hidden in the tumult of elephants, there was Maximus—flying. He had leapt off the rear of the plateau with his four limbs attached to his giant red cape that was now filled with air as he glided down to the back of the horseshoe plateau where Matthias was tied to the tree. Even the guards of the little boy cat had left their positions and ventured to the front of the stronghold to see the moving cloud. Maximus landed upright on his rear legs. With a swipe he cut the rope.

The boy cat hugged his uncle. "I knew you'd come."

Maximus lifted the boy cat to the back of his wide neck and said, "Put both paws around my neck and hold tight. This ride is not over yet."

As he said it, the first eyes of the enemy had turned to notice him. A voice shouted, "Look! He is there!"

From the tower, Reltih screamed, "Attack him!"

The forces ran toward Maximus. The giant cat waited for them to be almost upon him, then he made a burst forward and leaped a hundred feet over the horde, landing on the other side of them. The narrow entrance was ahead and now Reltih's forces were behind Maximus instead of in front of him. He looked up and saw Reltih atop the plateau. Reltih was waving his arm frantically. Maximus had no idea why but knew he had a clear path to the entrance and set off at as fast as he could run. Out of the corners of his eyes, Maximus saw two soldiers on the far right and left of him and in that split second they threw up their arms and a hidden rope came up that had been buried in the dirt. Maximus tried to hop over it and almost did but the rope caught his right back leg and he tumbled in a lump upon his face while Matthias still held tight.

The forces behind ran to catch up with the fallen giant. Maximus tried to get up and run. His leg gave way. It was broken. He tried to run on only three legs but this was too slow. The enemy was gaining. He was nearly at the opening. Yet, he knew that even if he got through it, Reltih's army would catch up to him and he would risk himself and Matthias. His mind called to the mind of the tiny sparrow that had seen all.

"Stephen, I cannot run. Lead Matthias out and take him to his father."

The sparrow asked, "But what of you, Maximus?"

Maximus glanced at the narrow opening and then said for the boy cat to hear. "I will block the entrance and prevent the soldiers from chasing after Matthias."

The boy cat was still wrapped around his uncle's neck and would not let go. "No, Maximus, I will not leave you." He began to cry.

"Matthias, there is no time to argue. Go with Stephen and I will follow after you, won't I Stephen?"

The sparrow knew that the giant cat he had promised to look after would not be able to follow them, but still he said, "Yes, Matthias, come quickly and Maximus will join us later."

The boy cat ran for the opening with Stephen on his shoulder.

Maximus called after them, "Stephen, return to tell me when the Matthias is safe."

Maximus crawled to the narrow opening. He made himself stand on his injured leg and filled the entrance with his great size. The enemy came. With the staff of Gerald, he swatted them like flies until they fell back, afraid of his might. From above, rocks were thrown, hitting and stunning Maximus. Even in his pain the falling rocks gave Maximus an idea. In that short moment when the soldiers in front of him retreated, Maximus took the rope from his right shoulder, looped one end and with the skill of years of practice, tossed it above, knocking off the stone thrower to his right. Then he threw the rope again and it caught the top off the scaffolding holding the rocks. He uncurled the rope from his left shoulder and repeated his throws to the left. Now he had hold of the scaffolds on both sides. He took each of the ropes into his right paw while he held fast to the staff with the left.

He pulled both ropes trying to bring down the scaffolds of rocks that would block the opening so that soldiers could not run after Matthias. The soldiers with only swords and clubs were afraid to come close to Maximus and his staff. Elegnam signaled from above and the archers and spear throwers advanced. They took aim while Maximus felt the injured leg giving way under his weight. He braced it even more but with greater difficulty. The spears and arrows flew towards him. He batted many away with the staff but some hit him and could be seen sticking from his giant body. These wounds were weakening him even more. The soldiers were moving closer and hitting their target more often.

With all of his might Maximus tried to pull down the stones that would block the entrance and save Matthias while still keeping off the enemy with his staff. One giant paw was not enough and the soldiers were getting closer. He would need both of his mighty arms. This would mean dropping the staff and spreading his arms wide to pull the ropes with all of his strength. Yet, if he did, his white chest would be an open target for the arrows and spears. He had no choice. He could not keep them away much longer. Maximus dropped the staff and with his arms stretched to each side, he pulled with all his remaining strength. The arrows and spears entered him and filled his chest until he looked like a porcupine. The enemy came closer as Maximus appeared to weaken. His injured leg buckled and he nearly fell forward. He was on one knee, nearly beaten. Maximus looked through his blurry eyes and the enemy seemed to be moving in slow motion as hazy figures closing ever nearer to the wounded giant.

He was nearly defeated but Matthias was not yet safe. With all of his great heart Maximus summoned his remaining strength. He stood straight up and, looking fiercely at his advancing enemies, roared his last great roar. The enemy for a moment froze. Maximus pulled the ropes. The scaffolding creaked and teetered. The soldiers looked up. From above Reltih and Elegnam screamed, "Hurry! Hurry!"

The arrows and spears flew hitting the open target. Maximus took a great breath and yanked with all the might he had left. The scaffolds gave way and the rain of rocks came down, blocking the opening as Maximus had wanted. No one would be going in or out anytime soon. Some of the stones struck Maximus and knocked him to the ground. He didn't care. Matthias was safe. He knew for sure when he saw above him the yellow dart and it was confirmed when he could hear Reltih yowl in frustration.

Maximus rolled onto his back to lessen the pain of the spears and arrows that had struck his chest. Now facing skyward, Maximus could see his old friend circling above him. From high up, Stephen's mind said to the mind of Maximus, "Huxley, Leopardus, and the Riders have Matthias and they are on the way here. The elephants are near and wait for your orders."

Huxley and his fellows arrived and joining the elephants, Huxley anxiously shouted, "Maximus!" But his best friend was too weak to answer from inside the stronghold.

Maximus, severely wounded, thought: What orders? The fact that the rocks prevented Reltih's forces to get out until they were cleared also meant that no one else could get in. "Stephen, tell them there is nothing they can do for me. They must save themselves, return to Catland, and organize to defeat Reltih."

As he said it, Reltih and Elegnam descended from the tower and Maximus could see them leading the soldiers cautiously toward him. Maximus could only move his eyes. The rest of his body was too weak and broken. Indeed, this body was almost used up and it was nearly time for his spirit to leave it.

His eyes saw the glee in the faces of Reltih and Elegnam. Reltih cackled, "Maximus is ours now, either alive as a slave, or stuffed and sold as a prize to the highest bidder."

The forces were nearly upon the giant cat, as he lay helpless in the bright sun that hurt his eyes. He tried to raise his paw to shield his eyes but was too weak even for that.

Outside, the allies of Maximus waited. Then their eyes turned skyward with amazement.

As if Max's wish for shade was heard, the day suddenly became as dark as a moonless and starless night. Reltih and his forces were crying out in fright. "What happened to the sun?"

Above them an immense dark brown cloud came closer and all could feel the powerful rush of a downward flowing wind. The cloud was the shape of a giant arrow. At the point of this arrow there was a red head topped with a red plume.

Wystan the Wise could fly again.

And thousands of eagles of Eagleland were with him.

Wystan's left wing pointed down. Half of the triangle flew toward Reltih and his forces. At this sight, they ran for their lives to hide. The flying squadron returned to its other half. With his right wing Wystan pointed to Maximus. He and one hundred of the eagles descended to the giant cat. Wystan alighted on Max's shoulder and said to him, "I have come for you my first son."

The great eagle shook his head as he looked at Max's white chest now nearly all red from his wounds. He signaled to the hundred eagles and said to them, "Come, make him pure again as he has always been and shall always be."

The eagles pulled out the arrows and spears and cleaned his wounds. When they finished, they rose from him and his white chest gleamed again. Wystan called for more eagles to descend and to Maximus he said, "It is time to take you home."

The many eagles circled Maximus and with their talons took secure hold of the cat's red cape. Now the cape was a cradle. They gently lifted Maximus off the ground, headed skyward, and flew him out of the enemy stronghold. The giant brown cloud followed this honor guard until they all reached Huxley, Matthias, and the Princess in the open plain. She had come at the summons of Stephen the Sparrow. The eagles laid Maximus down so Huxley and Matthias could see him once again. Max's time in this body was nearly gone. Wystan still sat on Max's shoulder and Huxley said to the great eagle, "Thank you, old friend."

At the sound of Huxley's voice, Maximus opened his eyes and he whispered, "Yes, Huxley, it certainly is a day for old friends to meet again."

Huxley took Max's paw in his paw and on the other side of the giant cat Princess took the other paw. Maximus asked her, "Is Matthias safe and well?"

She answered, "See for yourself," and the boy cat came and pressed his sorrowful face into the cheek of his uncle and said to him. "I don't want you to leave us."

Stephen the Sparrow hovered just above them. Seeing him made the Princess think of Gerald and she said to Maximus that she wished he were here.

Stephen giggled in his silly, high-pitched voice, which then turned into Gerald's voice. "But I have always been here." Then the little sparrow turned into the old sage with the blue eyes so that now Gerald and not the sparrow stood before them. Gerald told the Princess, "Did you think I would ever really leave you—or any of you?"

Maximus, with his eyes, motioned Gerald to bend his head to the giant cat's mouth. "Take back your staff, Gerald, I will not need it."

Gerald took it and promised, "Someday Maximus, when he is ready, I will give it to Matthias."

Huxley knew Max's time had come. He squeezed the great paw. "Maximus, I have loved you as if you were really my brother."

Then Wystan the Wise revealed the truth. "Huxley, you do not need to say 'as if' he is your brother,' for Maximus is your brother. Your mother was captured by Reltih and taken to the terrible cave. She would not be a slave so she willed herself to the Great Mystery, but just before she left her body she gave birth to Maximus and gave him to me to be found by your father."

This happy revelation gave some joy to this otherwise sad moment.

Huxley said to Maximus, "If only our father could know."

The eagle answered, "He does know. In searching for Maria, Trevenen knew a terrible grief that was unbearable. The Great Mystery saw his pain and took him to be with her again. They now wait for Maximus and for all of you when the time comes."

Matthias then asked the wise eagle, "Does this mean that we will all see Maximus again some day."

"Yes, Matthias," Wystan replied, "but you do not have to wait for the future to see him. Whenever you close your eyes and think of the Great Mystery, Maximus will be with you."

Maximus said to his beloved nephew, "So then there is no need to be sad for me Matthias, for now I will go to the Great Mystery and be at peace. I may leave this body but I will never leave you or your father and mother or Catland. My spirit will always be watching and if I am ever needed again, my spirit will enter a new body and return."

Then the eyes in the body of the giant cat closed for the last time.

The elephants with their trunks took hold of the red cape. Maximus would be returned to his home—Catland.

When the procession reached the river near the bridge, the citizens of Catland were all gathered. Many had never seen elephants. Yet, if they were led by Huxley and carrying Maximus, they could only be friends.

Huxley asked the elephants to lay Maximus at that part of the river where he, Maximus, and Princess had played as kittens. The citizens gathered and all purred so that the sound would carry high above and summon the Great Mystery. With them were the elephants and eagles led by Wystan. Clouds gathered and they all saw lightning followed by the sound of thunder.

A hole appeared in the cloud swirling mightily, and from this hole streaks of the lightning struck the ground around Maximus and little fires circled him. From the vortex in the clouds appeared a blue light and it reached down as a wide band to enter the circle of flames. The blue light sparkled and danced while appearing to surge upward. The blue was the same blue of Gerald's eyes and from his eyes the identical streaks of light met the magnificent band of light from the sky and they intersected where Maximus rested in the circle of fire.

At the point where the two bands of blue light met there was a bursting flash of white and a darker blue orb dashed up the vertical band of light and flew through the vortex in the sky. The spirit of Maximus had returned to where it had always been—in the Great Mystery.

The bands of blue light went with him, the circle of flame extinguished, and the ground within that circle was now empty.

Then Matthias pointed to the sky. When the lightning would strike, and for a mere second illuminate the dark clouds, behind them they could see in those brief flashes Maximus floating above them, his great red cape billowing in the sky. And then seconds later they saw Trevenen and Maria.

And so Grandpa Huxley finished telling the story of Maximus the First to Maximus the Second while Huxley's son Matthias listened. The bespectacled old cat said to his grandson, "So you see little one, there is no reason to be sad that I am leaving this body. For when I do, I will join your Great Uncle and the Princess once again." Then Huxley took off his lunettes. "I will not need these there. Go now little Maximus with your father. Let me close these old eyes. Go up the watch tower and wait." Matthias and Maximus the Second hugged Huxley's body for the last time and went outside. They climbed up the tower where Huxley had looked for his brother so many years before.

The thunder and lightning came again just as Grandpa Huxley had told in his story. The circle opened in the sky and whirled. The blue band of light came down and entered Huxley's burrow. A second later the darker blue orb flew up the band of light. The lights went back through the hole and the hole closed but the dark clouds remained with the thunder and lightning.

And there, behind the clouds during the flashes, Matthias and his son could see Huxley, Maximus, and Princess Blue as kittens again, playing by the river.

Thirty Years Later:
• • • • • • • • • • • • • • • •

Maximus the Second walked with his son, Huxley the Third, holding the boy cat's paw in his paw while he held the staff of Gerald in the other. After a long peace, the son of Reltih now threatened Catland in the same pattern as his father had done before. Maximus the Second was the leader of the Cat Council. He walked with his son to the bridge by the river to wait for the Freedom Riders to return from a rescue mission. They crossed the bridge and one of the Riders carried about his neck a sack. This Rider gently put the sack on the ground.

Maximus the Second approached the sack and opened it. "Look here, my son, see what I have found."

Out crawled this near-starved kitten whose fur was thin and sparse showing the rib bones that had not any fat whatsoever. As weak and skinny as he was, the kitten was already longer than the older Huxley the Third and his shoulders and hips were broader though there was hardly a muscle to be seen on them.

Huxley the Third put his twitching nose to the ground and approached the poor orphan. Their noses rubbed and the black and white little one reminded Huxley of his mother. Huxley licked the skin and bones and the kitten purred for the first time since leaving the side of Wystan the Wise. "Father," Huxley sighed, "he is so weak, the poor thing." And Huxley tried to lift him with his teeth by his neck as his father and especially his mother had done when Huxley was very little. The black and white kitten was too heavy, and Maximus the Second completed the task and carried him to their burrow.

The little orphan had very large and yellow eyes that were vibrant and alive and much more so than the rest of him. With these eyes he gazed at Huxley the Third until they were intently looking at each other. Then the black-backed cat winked.

You can only imagine what happens next.

Purring Heights

There are no ordinary cats. — Collette

Part One:

A Night at the Movies
••••••••••••••••••••

Sarah and John Fiore live in a two-story townhouse on Bleecker Street in New York City's Greenwich Village. Across the road is the *Happy Cat Boutique* with its pink neon sign flashing on and off. It's a store for cat lovers to spoil their cats with gourmet food, toys, pillows, videos, and clothes and jewelry for the cats' staff—meaning the humans that cats let own them. Sarah had adopted her now one-year old cat Cathy from the *Happy Cat Boutique* when she was 3 months old. Cathy was a moggie (mutt for dogs) and she was an unknown combination of maybe Persian, Siamese, and black/gray tabby around her face with black paws, but mainly solid gray from the neck back to her very fluffy tail, which was always standing straight up because she is a very happy cat. Cathy had amazing blue eyes and purred constantly. Sarah and John loved her madly. She was named after "Cathy" in Sarah's favorite novel *Wuthering Heights*. Sarah said that their townhouse home was *Purring Heights*. She even painted a sign that said Purring Heights and hung it on the front door.

The Happy Cat Boutique had a big screen TV in the store window facing Bleecker Street that showed cat movies and videos 24 hours a day, even when the store was closed. Many evenings, Sarah would sit by the front window while Cathy reclined on the windowsill and they both watched the big screen. *Stuart Little* was a favorite.

Sarah is British and a third grade teacher nearby. John is a sportswriter for New York *Newsday* so he was often not home until late as he was covering games. John covered the New York Mets, New York Knicks, and his favorite team, the New York Jets. Sarah really wasn't a big sports fan, proving opposites do attract. When he wasn't home Sarah and Cathy would hang out by the window and watch the shows across the street in the Happy Cat Boutique. There was one of those electric signs in the window like the crawl on the bottom of the news on TV that gave the schedule and names of the films that would be showing. At 8:15 the next show would be the movie *The Adventures of Milo and Otis*. Lately, there was a second unexpected show on the sidewalk and on the cars parked next to the sidewalk.

Tonight, like the previous two nights, a second audience came to see the movies in the store window. At about 8 P.M. on this summer evening little shadows began to appear strolling on the sidewalk from under the streetlight to the right of the cat store; these were little shapes that glided silently and unseen—except by Cathy and Sarah. There was a white one, a calico one, a charcoal gray one, many different colors as could be dimly seen by the streetlight above them. Each began to jump on the two cars directly in front of the big TV, nine in all. They sat, or stretched out across the roofs of the two cars, all facing the TV.

Three stores to the right of the cat boutique was Benny's Bagels. At 8:05 from the narrow alley next to Benny's one more shape emerged—another cat with something in his mouth that was as big as the head that held it. The object was round with a hole in the middle. That cat was a butterscotch and cream tabby but instead of stripes he had swirls; he looked like a cinnabun. His full name is Butterscotch Trublay (AKA trouble), which he was always getting into. His cat pals call him BT.

As BT got closer to the cat store, Sarah could see that the shape in his mouth was a bagel. (Benny was a sucker for cats and left bagels for them at night.) From the left a giant cat—a black and white Tuxedo cat that looked like Sylvester—jogged up to BT. He is huge—more than twice as big than the average cat and larger even than some dogs. When he got to BT, this giant, called Dead Ahead Fred (how he got this name is a story to be told later) snapped at the bagel in BT's mouth and grabbed it in his big fangs. They appeared to be wrestling for it and pulled at it wildly. Sarah and Cathy thought that the much smaller butterscotch cat didn't have a chance.

Still, the giant cat did not tear the bagel away but just pulled until the bagel tore in two with one half in each cat's mouth. Then this duo jumped on one car each and shared the bagel with the other cats. Sarah was fascinated, almost in a trance, watching what had looked like a fight turn into feast. At precisely 8:15, the eating stopped and all sat up at attention in front of the screen. The cats acted as if they knew it was time for *The Adventures of Milo and Otis* to begin.

For the next hour and a half, the cats on the cars and the cat in the window with Sarah watched the movie. When the movie ended, the cats jumped down from the cars and walked back to the alley next to Benny's Bagels where they disappeared into the darkness. Sarah went to bed and Cathy settled next to her between her arm and her torso where Sarah petted her over and over until Cathy purred herself to sleep.

John came home after midnight. He came to bed and Sarah told him about the events of the evening. He thought she was joking.

"Really, John, they were watching the movie!"

"Maybe it was just a big coincidence?"

"No way! This has happened three nights in a row and maybe longer, but we only started paying attention since Monday night."

"We?"

"Me and Cathy," and just then Cathy wakened to John's voice, yawned, and rolled over to his side to get petted and John was happy for his little girl to purr some more.

"John, try to come home early one night and you'll see them."

"I'll try soon."

"And also try to give the truck a start; we never use it and it needs to run once in a while." The car was parked behind their townhouse but subways and busses were easier so the truck didn't move much.

"Will do!"

The Cat Gang

•••••••••••••

Meanwhile, back in the alley:

The ten cats had settled under an awning over the back door of Benny's Bagels. Benny stuck his head out the back door and smiled at his cat pals. He laid some bagels and cream cheese down on a paper plate and went back in. The cats scrambled after their food and then got ready for naptime. They were a cat gang. BT was the brain of the operation and Dead Ahead Fred was the muscle. Not that Fred wasn't smart, but BT had a creative imagination, which could be either a good thing or a bad thing depending on the particular situation he was getting himself into. The ten cats banded together because there were dogs out there with an attitude but none that would mess with ten cats, especially if one was Fred. Fred had clobbered some big poochies and the rest were very careful not to annoy him. He would avoid a fight if it only involved him, but he would not let anyone pick on his smaller friends. His best friend is BT who likes to tease dogs because he can get away with it with Fred around. Fred is a giant with a heart of gold—and a sucker for BT's schemes

The ten cats besides BT and Fred are Tarzan, the calico cat who had a stopwatch tied around his neck, Snowball, the white cat, Bogey, a black and white striped Tabby, Cleopatra (Cleo for short), a black and gold girl cat, Dandy, who was BT's brother and the same color, Sherlock, who was Bogey's brother, and another clever fellow like BT, Emma, a Persian beauty and a matchmaker, and last, but not least, old Eric, the ancient and wise father figure to them all who was jet black with large yellow eyes that seemed to glow in the dark.

The "terrible ten," as BT had named them were now nine—BT had gone for a walk.

The cats were asleep but Eric lifted his left ear and then said to Fred next to him, "BT's on the road again."

"Whaddya think he's up to?"

"Don't know, but with BT, we better keep our eyes and ears on steady alert or we'll have another Jeep incident."

Fred said, "yuck," and made a face. "Don't remind me!"

The Jeep Incident

• • • • • • • • • • • • • • • •

The "Jeep incident" was a BT brainstorm with some fur-raising results.

About six months earlier BT was in charge of supplies. This meant he scouted the neighborhood to see where the gang could get useful stuff like a variety of food (can't eat bagels all the time), cardboard boxes (to crawl into), fresh water, (puddles are not always healthy), towels (blankets for cold days), and whatever BT could think of, including reading material about cats; BT particularly liked Aldous Huxley's essay "Sermons in Cats," where the author tells a young writer to learn about people by watching cats first.

One day, BT made a really good find. He was able to sneak into a local food market's storeroom through the delivery entrance and found the boxes of cat food. He could tear one open and eat some but could only manage to cart off a single box at a time and with great difficulty. The rest of the gang could help but they would be too easily spotted as a group. So BT was dragging one box in his teeth and was complaining to himself the whole time. Then he passed a Toys 'R Us. Outside, a salesman was demonstrating a miniature Jeep for a dad and the dad's eight-year-old boy who was in the driver's seat and making circles in the parking lot. BT dropped the box and ran back to bagel alley.

The gang was lounging out as BT ran and slid right up to Fred's sleepy head.

"Yo, y'all, get up off your lazy tails and follow me!" BT did a U-turn and headed back to Toys 'R Us.

The terrible nine followed BT, trying to keep up. BT was very athletic and the fastest runner in the gang. Eric told him God made him fast because he was always running away from trouble. BT leaped on the hood of an old blue Cadillac and the gang took up positions around him.

"Look!" The little boy was still driving the mini Jeep.

Sherlock: "At what?"

BT: "That pink thing with the kid in it."

Bogey: "Fred, I don't like what I'm seeing; talk to the boy genius before somebody gets hurt."

Fred: "Okay BT what are we doing here?"

BT: "I'm the supply guy right!"

Fred: "Yeah!"

BT: "Well instead of just dragging around one thing at a time, we could use that pink machine to haul lots of stuff."

Tarzan was the car expert. He knew just how fast a car could go and how long it took a car to brake at any speed so that street crossing was now a science and not just a guessing game. This is why he has the stopwatch at all times. "That 'pink machine' is a battery-operated toy version of a Jeep Cherokee."

BT: "Whatever! I want it!"

Dandy: "To haul stuff?"

BT: "Yeah!"

Emma the Matchmaker cooed and fluttered her long white eyelashes, "I think BT wants it to get girls."

Cleo: "Emma's right BT, we're not stupid. We've seen car commercials on TV."

BT stood upright crossed his front paws over his chest and made his most pathetic pouting face, acting greatly offended.

Fred: "Puleasssssse! Enough with the face. And like you have never been interested in girls. How many times have I had to save you from jealous boyfriends?"

And the rest of the gang went, "uh huh," and rapidly shook their heads up and down in agreement with Fred.

BT: "That's all in the past. I'm more mature now."

This response was met with nine faces of disbelief.

BT: "Really! I just want that Jeep for us," BT rubbed his paws, "and think of all the goodies we could carry!"

Eric: "And how do you intend to get it?"

"We'll get over close to it and wait for the kid to get out."

Fred was alarmed; he knew what "we" meant. "And what happens when the kid gets out?"

"We jump in and drive off with it."

Snowball: "I see only one little problem. . . . None of us knows how to drive."

BT: "How hard could it be if the kid could do it? Whaddaya think Tarzan, you're the car expert."

"I time 'em; I don't drive 'em. Let's look inside this blue Caddy we're sitting on." The group moved closer to the windshield, Tarzan first. He got right up to the glass.

"There's that round thing that makes the wheels turn." Tarzan climbed on the Caddy's roof and hung over the driver's side window hanging from his back paws. "There's something in the middle between the front seats—have no clue what it is."

On the floor under the round thing are two pedals. Since all cars just do three things—stop, start, turn—the round thing must steer, and the pedals must make it go and stop—don't ask me which does what."

BT: "What about going backwards?"

"Maybe that's what the thing in the middle is for." Tarzan then flipped himself back on the roof and then down to the hood, facing the rest. "Guessing is not the same as knowing."

Fred: "That's right BT; what we don't know won't hurt us and we don't need to learn."

"But Fred, think of all the Temptations Turkey Treats we could haul."

These were Fred's favorite snack. Just the thought made him lick his lips with his giant cat tongue.

BT pointed at Fred and said to the gang, "There, see! And how about you Snowball? Thinking about tuna? And Cleo, you never get enough shrimp."

The gang was now all dreaming of goodies with visions over their heads.

BT knew he was on a roll. "So whaddya say Gang?"

He really meant Fred. Fred always did the dangerous stuff. He didn't want anyone else getting hurt. Fred looked at all these happy cat faces dreaming of their favorite foods and gave in.

"OK, wise guy, what's the plan?"

From somewhere BT suddenly had on big black sunglasses and produced a pair for Fred. "Put these on!"

Fred hesitated. "What for?"

"Conceal our identities."

Fred rolled his eyes. "But we're cats." Nonetheless, Fred put them on. Once BT got an idea in his head, it wasn't worth trying to talk him out of it.

Fred and BT slowly strolled towards the Pink Jeep, still being driven by the boy. They got very low to the ground like cats do when hunting (or spying) and worked their way to the Chevy truck nearest to the jeep. Trucks were good for cats because they had higher ground clearance to run under. Tarzan had measured every truck because only the most clearance would be enough for big Freddie to go under. The Chevy was high enough. The remaining cats remained on the blue Caddy and became an audience for BT's latest adventure.

The little boy finally came to a stop and got out of the pink Jeep. The dad and the salesman were talking with their backs to the machine. Fred and BT streaked out from under the Chevy and leaped into the Jeep. Fred was at the wheel; BT was down by the two pedals. The Jeep started to slowly roll on its own a few feet from the salesman who finally noticed and yelled: "Hey!"

BT still didn't know what to do so Fred stuck his big leg out the side and was pushing like he was on a skateboard. The jeep rolled faster. The salesman started going after them. "BT, do something!"

"I don't know which one makes it go."

"Pick one!"

BT jumped on the left one. The Jeep stopped short and Fred went half over the wheel onto the hood and roared "Dat ain't it!"

The salesman was near the back bumper. BT leaped to the right pedal and the Jeep took off. Fred was back behind the wheel trying to steer. First he did a wheelie to the left then he made a wheelie to the right with the salesman trying to keep up. BT was bouncing around down below and Fred was swinging from the wheel, barely holding on. The Jeep was aimed straight ahead towards the cat audience. Fred froze. The cats on the blue Chevy were yelling, "Here comes Fred, dead ahead. Turn! Turn!" Their eyes were big as cups. They leaped in all directions. Emma and Cleo leaped on the nearest tree trunk and speeded up out of harm's way and on to a branch. Both looked down. A crash was next. They covered their eyes.

Fred: "BT, do da brake!"

BT jumped back on the brake. The jeep stopped short. Fred bounced over the wheel again but didn't let go of it, then fell back into the seat. He heard BT from below, "Turn right!" Fred rolled the wheel to the right. BT jumped back on the go pedal and the jeep headed for the parking lot exit, the salesman losing ground. Fred turned left at the exit with the cat gang right behind. At Bleecker and Morton they passed some dogs from Bowser's gang. BT yelled over, "Bet you want wanna these." The dogs growled and took a few steps until Fred snarled a big fang at them. The poochies retreated. Then the gang finally made it back to Benny's alley.

Fred was still frozen at the wheel. BT shakily emerged from below, wobbling out of the Jeep.

BT regained his cool and said to Frozen Fred, "It woulda been a breeze if you knew how to drive."

The gang laughed in big hee-haws. Old Eric remembered the sight of the pink Jeep flying straight for the blue Caddy at top speed and said, "From now on big buddy your name is Dead Ahead Fred."

This caused lots more big hee-haws from the gang. Fred was not happy.

Fred's head turned towards BT's face. Fred's very long fangs were in attack mode and he was growling. BT had seen those fangs in action and started to back up. Fred stood up and through those fangs whispered, "I'm gonna kill you."

BT leaped in reverse and took off. Fred went after him. Like Eric said God made BT fast so he could run away. Fred didn't kill him but he got his new nickname from this adventure.

But BT did turn out to be right. Wow, could they haul stuff in that pink Jeep.

The Girl
• • • • • • • •

"Yeah, big Freddie," Eric said back in the present, BT's been on the prowl lately. I think our pal Trublay has been bitten again."

"Whaddya mean, bitten?"

"He's been taking walks for a while same time every night. Cleo followed him last night, and . . ."

"And what?"

"You know BT."

"Oy, not again!"

"I'm afraid so big buddy. He's been bitten by the love bug. There's a girl involved."

"Well," Fred said, "we'll just have to wait and see."

With that Fred and old Eric put their heads down, closed their eyes and dreamed of catnip mice.

Yes, Fred and Eric did know BT. The butterscotch cinnabun was standing in front of the Happy Cat Boutique looking up at a lighted window. When the light went out, BT crossed the street and climbed a tree up to the second-floor height. A long branch nearly touched the now dark window. BT carefully tip-pawed along the branch. At the end of the branch, BT leaped to the windowsill. Inside, in the dark, Cathy was waiting.

BT and Cathy nuzzled their noses against the glass.

The next morning was a Saturday:

The Paper Boy
• • • • • • • • • • • • •

Sarah sleepily put on her cat slippers, and her cat bath-robe to go get the paper. She opened the front door with a big yawn. Her mouth stayed open wide when a butterscotch tabby tried to run past her to get in the house. She barely closed the door in time. Sarah looked through the peephole. No cat. She opened the door again. The cat tried to get in again. She closed the door in his face.

She called to upstairs. "John!"

Mr. Groggy-voice answered, "What?"

"I can't get the paper."

That seemed odd.

"Why not?" Isn't it there?"

"Yes . . . but . . . "

"But what?"

"There's cat out there that's trying to get in the house and I can't get the paper."

"Shoo it away!"

Silence.

"I get it; you want me to do it." John moped down the stairs. He looked through the peephole. "No cat now."

She said, "He's sneaky!"

"Why the heck does he want to come in here? He probably heard that you're a sucker for cats."

She didn't deny it.

John wanted his paper so he could read his sports column in it. He went to the coat closet and got a broom.

"Oh, John, don't hit him."

"Would I do that? I'll just block him off with it. Don't forget that I used to be a hockey goalie."

Maybe so but he had never faced a puck like BT.

He opened the door. BT dashed. John blocked. BT had more moves than a slinky, but John held him off. John exclaimed, "This cat's got more moves than Curtis Martin." Martin is a running back for the New York Jets. Finally, John pushed BT back enough to get the paper and run back inside while Sarah closed the door, which BT smacked into with a sharp thud.

On the inside, John said, "What was that about?" Then he went into the kitchen to get coffee and read the paper.

That night BT made his tree climb and tightrope walked to Cathy's dark window. He jumped to the window box. Cathy was waiting. BT said, "What's up Girly?" Their noses nuzzled against the glass. Cathy said, "I have an idea."

Sunday morning:
· · · · · · · · · · · · · · · · ·

Sarah went down for the paper in her cat robe and slippers. She looked through the peephole. The butterscotch cat was there and she couldn't believe what he was doing.

BT was somehow holding the paper between his teeth like a dog would.

"John."

"Yeah."

"He's back!"

"Who? The Terminator?"

"Very funny! No the cat. Come down, you need to see this."

John got the broom again.

"No, don't do that. Look through the door first."

He did. "Holy Moley!"

He put his hand on the doorknob.

"John, wait! If you go out there, he might run off with the paper."

Not a good thing. John cannot start his day without coffee and the newspaper.

"Alright," he said, "I'll do it very slowly."

John went out the door gently. For every step John took forward, the cat backed up just as far, keeping the same distance between them.

"Nice kitty, isn't that paper heavy; don't you just want to drop it?"

BT bit the paper harder.

John called back to Sarah, "He's not giving it up."

Sarah had often thought that Cathy should have a cat playmate. Maybe this was an omen that Cathy would get one now. "Well honey," she said, "I guess no paper for you today."

"No way!" John lunged at the paper. BT retreated a few feet but then stopped and he and John had a stare-down.

"John, you're starting to look a little ridiculous."

He pouted like a little boy. "I want my paper!"

Sarah smiled, "Well, I guess you're just going to have to let him in."

John surrendered. He backed up into the house and held the door wide open. BT didn't hesitate and ran in, dropping the paper on the floor and flying up the stairs as Cathy met him half way down. BT sniffed her ear and said, "Hello Girly!" The cats super-nuzzled and rolled around with each other; then they ran up to Cathy's room.

Sarah and John stood with their mouths open and suspicious faces.

John folded his arms very sternly across his chest like a puzzled dad would. "Is there a conspiracy going on here? . . . Sarah, did you have anything to do with this?"

"No way!"

For the rest of the day Sarah and John were greatly entertained by two very happy cats running, jumping, playing, and snuggling. That night Sarah, John, Cathy, and BT went to sleep together on the big king-sized bed.

John asked Sarah, "What are we going to call him?"

"Well, Cathy is Cathy like in *Wuthering Heights*, soooo-ooo . . ."

He laughed. "Heathcliff!"

And that's how BT got his new name.

Football Fans

Two months later—Sunday afternoon:
• •

John quickly learned that there was one great advantage of having Heathcliff around. Every day John would open the front door and BT would get the morning paper and bring it in. Once Sarah wondered if she and John should worry about Heathcliff getting tempted to run away.

John laughed. "Are you kidding? He's living in cat heaven. Great food, loving parents and he's nuts about Cathy and she's nuts about him." John was right. BT wasn't going anywhere. But this didn't mean he didn't miss his other life and he certainly missed the gang.

After getting his paper, John saw an article about petnappers. It seemed that there were some people out there stealing dogs and cats from their owners' homes. He said nothing to

Sarah because it would upset her. He did mention to always keep the kids locked in.

At noon John was in position in the living room. This meant he was stretched in front of the big screen TV on his armchair, legs extended over the footrest. He had popcorn and chips on a table and was watching the Jets pre-game show—one minute to game time. A second smaller chair was on the other side of the table. John wore his green Jets jersey with number 12 on it and the name of his favorite player, Jet quarterback, Joe Broadway. In John's imagination he daydreamed about being the Jets quarterback himself. He had played quarterback in high school. Sarah was in the kitchen.

John called out from his chair, "What are you kids doing in there?"

Sarah was standing over a counter cutting vegetables. "We're getting lunch ready for halftime."

"We?"

"Sure, Cathy is supervising from her management perch." Cathy was in a basket that was hardly big enough so she would curl into it with her head kind of hanging off the side. She gave a squeak as if to answer her dad, to which John replied. "Good girl Cathy, keep mom in line and on time."

Sarah laughed, "Gee, thanks!"

The game was about to start. John alerted his game-watching partner. "Heathcliff, it's starting."

Heathcliff—AKA BT—ran in from the bedroom with his little green Jet helmet and a jersey just like John's. His pointed ears stuck out through holes in the top. He leaped into the second chair and sat just like John did. John had wanted to get Cathy a cheerleader's outfit but Sarah had her limits.

The game began. The boys were totally focused on the TV. The girls watched from the kitchen. Sarah said to Cathy. "Look, sweetie, sports and food, that's all we need for those silly boys." Cathy squeaked.

This was the Jets fourth game of the season. The team had one win, two losses and needed to get better soon or the season would be lost. Joe Broadway hadn't been playing well. The boys in the chairs were very tense on every single play. The girls could hear them moan or yell at every play and see them make faces of either joy or pain. The Jets were marching on the other team and looked like they would score but Joe Broadway threw an interception.

The boys covered their eyes and yelled "Not again!" Three hours later, the Jets had lost. Sarah came out and said she was sorry that the Jets lost but that the boys could not get into a mopey funk for the rest of the day. They did their best to be cheerful.

That's So Romantic
• • • • • • • • • • • • • • • • • •

After Sarah and John went to sleep, Cathy and Heathcliff sat on the windowsill where BT first met her. They did this most nights often with Sarah. They all watched the nightly cat show in front of the Happy Cat Boutique. BT missed his friends and his life outside but he knew that he couldn't give up Cathy. He told her again about the first time he saw her.

"Yeah Fred and I were driving the pink Jeep at night after a pick up of supplies. Fred was out of Temptations Turkey

Treats and he is not fit to live with when he doesn't have them. It's like an obsession. Well, we were passing The Happy Cat Boutique and I happened to look up. One window had a light on and you were sitting in it. The light made your fur shine like a halo. After that, I was like Fred—obsessed."

Cathy fluttered her long eyelashes. "That's so romantic. And I have a confession to make. I had seen you outside before that night and I was sitting in the window hoping you would come by."

"Really!" Then he blushed.

Cathy said, "You are such a big sugar cube. You act like you're such a tough cat but you're really just a big catnip mouse." BT was tough, but also sweet. Eric would always say that "what matters most is how you see yourself" and that when BT saw his reflection, he didn't see a cat but a lion that came to save the day.

They held paws. BT looked out the window. "Someone's coming."

Out on that branch that BT had climbed when he met Cathy came Cleo for a visit.

Cleo and the other cats—except one—came by often to say hello.

Cleo reported on the gang's activities. Mainly she told them how much they all missed BT, and even how they missed the mischief they'd get into because of BT.

BT asked, "Fred still driving the Jeep?"

"Yes," said Cleo, "Tarzan and Bogey take turns being the pedal cats."

"How's my brother?"

"Misses you."

Tell him and the rest of the gang I miss them too."

Then BT raised a sore point. "How's Fred?"

"The same. Protects all of us from mean dogs and petnappers."

Fred was the only cat that hadn't visited him. Cleo said it was because the skinny branch she was sitting on wouldn't hold such a giant cat. But BT thought it was something else. "Is he still mad that I left?"

Cleo didn't answer that question, which was answer enough, but she tried to cover it up. "Well, he's been worried lately because of those petnappers being around. Fred even made a truce with Bowser's dog gang so we could look out for each other."

"Good idea, even though I hate them poochies."

Cathy shook her head. "No, you can't think that way. You've got to be like mom and love everyone."

"Easy for you to say. You're just like Mom."

"Well, you've gotten better. You don't scare the birds away anymore."

Cleo was amazed at this new attitude. "He doesn't?"

"No, now the three gray doves come sit on the sill and sing for us."

BT shrugged it off, "No big deal, besides, I've got big plans for those songbirds." The girls laughed. They assumed he was joking. Never assume with BT. Later that day BT began the birds' training. BT learned that their names were Maya, Virginia and Stormy.

For the Birds

A week later:
•••••••••••

Fred and the gang were in bagel alley. They were playing poker, using one of BT's cardboard boxes for a card table. Of course, they learned how from BT. Fred had on his sunglasses to hide his eyes so the other players couldn't read them. Bogey dealt the cards. Each cat player picked up his hand of cards or in this case his paw. Cleo and Emma were not interested in cards. They were getting sun.

As Fred was concentrating on his cards, he felt fluttering wings above him and saw three doves land on top of Benny's awning. The birds were cooing a sweet song. He didn't look up, but said, "Hey keep it down; I'm working here." The three doves flew down and landed on the card table. Their flapping wings blew the cards away. The players yelled at them and ran around chasing the cards.

Fred said, "Shoo," but they just kept sitting there.

One had something in its little beak. She dropped it on the table. Fred saw that it was a Temptations Turkey Bite. He knew BT had sent it.

Eric saw it too. "Well, Big Freddie, I think Trublay has sent you a peace offering." Fred grunted. Old Eric put his paw around Fred's shoulder. "Don't stay mad at him big boy. You know I always say that you can't control love but that you just have to flow with it. BT loves the girl; that doesn't mean he doesn't love you too and miss you."

Friends Again

· · · · · · · · · · · · ·

Fred grunted. But the next thing Eric knew the giant was climbing the tree trunk outside Cathy's window. Fred got to the right branch. He looked at it—kind of thin. He put one leg on it and bounced it a little, then a second leg, and slowly a third and fourth. He very slowly tight roped the skinny branch—skinny for his size anyway. He got to the window and tapped on the glass.

Cathy jumped on the sill first. She had never seen such a giant and her little mouth dropped open. "You must be Fred."

Fred said shyly, "Yup, that's me. Is BT around?"

Cathy answered, "I'm Cathy. He talks about you all the time."

"Really!"

"He misses you very much. I'll get him."

BT came to the window. The two buddies nuzzled through the glass.

"Thanks for coming big guy. I knew the turkey bite would get you."

You know me like a book. Can't resist that stuff. You doin' good?

"Yeah, but I miss all of you."

"Us too. Old Eric says it can't be helped."

"Old Eric is right. You still driving the Jeep?"

"Absolutely. It turned out to be a great idea—even if I didn't think so at the time."

BT laughed, "What was it you said? Something like, 'I'm gonna kill you.' I wish I had a piece of shrimp for every time you've said that to me."

"You could open a fish store. . . . I never meant it."

"I know big guy. Speaking of the Jeep, do you see that black pick-up truck by the fire hydrant?"

"Yeah."

"That's ours."

"Whaddya mean, ours?"

"It belongs to the people we let live here with us."

"Are they nice people?"

"Unbelievable. Cathy and I eat like we're the King and Queen."

"Maybe you will be someday, although I think you're more cut out to be the court jester."

"Very funny. Maybe we'll get to ride in that truck some-day."

"Would you drive?"

"I'd still want you to be the driver."

"No way! The pink jeep's enough but I'll take a look in it on the way down."

They both heard a crack. Fred's eye got big! "Which may be sooner than I was expecting." There was a second crack and the thin branch bent at an angle. Fred was backing up as fast as he could. The third crack was the charm. Down came the branch and Fred had his four legs stuck out while his back was heading to the dirt below.

Thud!

Fred was flattened in the dirt that was a cut out in the shape of Fred and his four flying legs.

BT yelled. "Are you okay?"

Fred stood up and with a big shake tossed off all the dirt on him and it went flying in all directions, including up at BT.

"Hey it wasn't my fault."

Fred answered, "BT, I'm gonna kill you." Just like old times. They were friends again.

Always
• • • • • • •

Later that night, John was packing a suitcase. He was going out of town to follow the New York Knicks while they played on the road. Sarah and the kids would miss him. He was a kid too—just a big one. Sarah was concerned about how much he was on airplanes. He knew it and would always reassure her that everything would be fine.

He knew by her face what she was thinking even if she didn't say it.

"Sarah, nothing will happen."

"I can't help worrying."

"I know but think of it this way. We are meant to be together. That will never change. Even if something did happen, we'd find each other again. I'll come back. I might be someone else, but I'll come back. Heck, I might even be a quarterback."

John hugged Sarah and said, "I will always love you."

The next morning John caught an early flight. The plane crashed, losing all on board. John's friend Martin who worked on the same newspaper came to tell Sarah. He left and she collapsed on the sofa and sobbed. Cathy and BT had heard what the visitor said and ran down the stairs. Each got on one side of their mom. She held them tight to her and kept crying.

Three weeks later—Monday morning:

Sarah had taken a leave of absence from her teaching job. Her third graders missed her. Sarah, Cathy and BT missed John. Sarah had no family here and was thinking about going back to England. Her friends at school tried to visit and keep her busy but they had their own lives to get back to and most of the time she was home alone with her cats. This was hard on her and her mind would drift into deep sadness sometimes; she would often forget things that needed to be done. The kids knew this was not like her at all. One day she forgot to put cat food out. BT raided the pantry and got the box out on his own. Cathy got a first look at BT's special skill in turning doorknobs. She had no idea that on the street BT had been the master cat burglar.

Sarah was still asleep. She slept a lot lately. The cats would try to wake her with meows, squeaks and kisses to her face. She'd open her eyes a little smile give each a quick stroke with her hand and then close her eyes again. The kids went down stairs to wait for the mail that would be dropped in through the mail slot in the front door. They would grip the mail in their teeth and bring it upstairs to Sarah. She would hardly look at the envelopes let alone open them and then threw them into a pile that was getting higher by the day.

Today, she forced herself to get up. Sarah had to go to the insurance company and get a check for John's life insurance. She hated even the thought of it because it was so final. Sarah came down the stairs in a trance. She took the garbage out the back door and then left through the front door, not even saying goodbye to the cats. Just inside the front door was a stack of newspapers. BT kept bringing the papers in but Sarah never

164 • *Maximus in Catland* and *Purring Heights*

read them. She had no idea what was going on in the world or in the country or in New York City or on Bleecker Street.

Leo and Lonnie: Petnappers

About noon the cats heard the backdoor open. Mom never came home through the backdoor. They realized that she had forgotten to lock it. Cathy and BT heard it open. Cats know when strangers are around by smell and by the sound and vibration of their footsteps. There were two and neither one was Sarah. BT put his paw to his mouth for quiet and led Cathy to the back of John's armchair where they hid.

A tall guy and a short guy entered the living room.

The tall one said, "Okay, Leo, you said that there was a gorgeous cat in here."

Cathy whispered, "Who are they?" BT knew they were the petnappers and that they were after Cathy. His little heart with the soul of a lion beat very fast.

"Yeah, Lonnie, she's got blue eyes and is absolutely adorable—super potential for cat commercials."

Leo and Lonnie were brothers even with the big difference in height. Lonnie was the brains. They both had on baseball caps that said, "L & L's Pet Stars." They ran a talent agency for animals. They were very particular when it came to finding pets that had the look advertisers wanted. In fact, if clients described a particular type of cat or dog that they wanted, Leo and Lonnie would scout around for the exact match, even if this meant catnapping or dognapping.

Leo and Lonnie looked around the living room. BT and Cathy would slide low on the floor and move behind another piece of furniture, always just a step ahead. Leo pulled a net from his coat pocket and held it wide between his outstretched hands.

BT knew that they couldn't do this hiding game forever. He said to Cathy, "You need to get upstairs and go out the window where the tree is and climb down; then go to Bagel alley."

"But aren't you coming?"

"I've got to distract them first. When I move, dash for the stairs. Don't think, just run!"

BT jumped from the floor to the top of John's armchair in plain sight.

Leo saw him first. "Hey Lonnie, there's one."

Lonnie looked, "He's not the girl, dummy."

"Yeah, but he's kind of cute too. Maybe we should take them both."

"Okay, but get we gotta get the girl first."

Leo moved towards the armchair, which was where Cathy was still hiding.

BT yelled, "Now!" Cathy took off for the stairs.

Leo saw her and turned to go after her.

BT leaped on to Leo's head and pulled his cap down over his eyes, then bit him on the nose. Leo screeched. Lonnie went after Cathy. BT let go of Leo and ran in front of Lonnie's legs tripping him so he fell flat on his face. Leo still couldn't see and fell over Lonnie.

Cathy was halfway up the stairs. BT yelled, "Keep going!"

Leo swiped at BT but missed him. Lonnie got up and was starting for the stairs.

Cathy was on the top landing; she was afraid for BT. BT jumped on the sofa then onto a bookcase and on to the steps ahead of Lonnie so that BT was face to face with the kitnapper. BT, in his mind's eye was that lion and out of his mouth came a lion's deafening roar. The brothers froze. BT yelled for Cathy to keep going. She went into the bedroom; she couldn't see what was happening outside on the stairs. She didn't want to leave BT and hesitated. BT turned to go after her. Lonnie recovered and grabbed BT's tail. BT's little feet were running in place but he couldn't get out of Lonnie's grip. BT was showing his fangs and growling. He wished Fred were here.

Then Lonnie lifted BT up by his tail and threw him against the wall. BT shrieked!

Cathy ran back out at the sound. Leo was waiting and threw the net over her, picked her up and the catnappers ran out the back door to a waiting van. BT had been stunned; he tried to get up but stumbled. He tried again and ran out just in time to see the van's back door closing. The van took off. BT ran after it, darting in and around traffic. The van was too fast but has to stop at a light with BT in pursuit. BT put his paw in his mouth and whistled. The three doves appeared.

"Maya and Virginia, Go get Fred and the gang! Tell them to go to the house. Stormy, go back to the house and get Sarah's car keys. Give them to Fred and tell him to drive the truck and follow me while I keep following Cathy."

The doves raced on their missions.

The Chase

· · · · · · · · · ·

On Bleecker Street the two doves flew out of Bagel Alley, and then charging out after them was the gang with Fred the giant in front. He had on his angry face, which meant all teeth showing and those long fangs in attack mode. Maya and Virginia led Fred to the car. Stormy was flying above it with the keys in her beak. Ginny told him that BT wanted him to drive after him.

Fred looked at the size of the truck and just shook his head. "You can't be serious!"

"Hey, I'm just doing what BT told me. BT said it's no different than the Jeep, just bigger."

"Yeah, just a little."

The three doves lined up in flight formation over the car.

Maya said, "Okay big boy, get in and start driving, then follow us."

Fred yelled for Bogey and Tarzan to be the pedal cats. They all jumped in the cab and the rest of the gang got in the back of the pick-up.

Fred got it started. A crash here and a crash there and the cats in the back were bouncing around while they tried to hang on for dear life. Fred finally got it out onto Bleecker Street and the chase began.

Fred was honking the horn. Other drivers wanted to see who the nut was. When the saw Fred, first they were in shock, then they made sure to get out of the way. There were a few more crashes.

One driver got on his cell phone and dialed 911.

The dispatcher asked what the emergency was.

"There's a cat driving a car down Bleecker Street."

"Sir do you know it is a crime to make a false report."

"But . . . but . . . "

The dispatcher hung up.

BT heard the honking as he was running after the van. His head turned like a swivel and his heart leaped when he saw Big Freddie at the wheel. He knew Bogey and Tarzan had a pedal each. Fred would yell, "Gas!" then "Brake!" while he tugged at the wheel. The truck would leap forward or come to a dead halt and then start over again. Fred, Bogey and Tarzan's coordination got better as they went along.

Fred saw the dove Maya flying next to BT's head. Then she flew to the truck. "He wants you to get beside him so he can jump in the cab." Fred pulled the black truck next to BT. Never mind the car he pushed out of the way to do it. BT leaped in, huffing and puffing. Fred still had the van in sight. BT caught his breath. "Catch up! Catch up!" Fred did the best he could. The cats were gaining on the van. Up ahead was a split in the road. Which way would the van go, left or right?

In the van Leo was driving. He looked in the rear view. "Yo, Lonnie we got a black truck after us."

"You sure!"

"Yeah!"

"Lose it."

Leo turned his cap around and stepped on it. Lonnie's neck snapped back and he hit his head on the back of the cab.

Fred said, "There's a split up ahead at Broadway and Seventh Avenue. I don't know which way they're gonna go." The van was on the right so Fred went right.

BT yelled, "I'm getting on the roof."

Fred said, "Are you nuts, what the heck for?"

"I'm gonna be ready to jump from here to the van if I have to."

Fred: "Ohhhhhhhh myyyyyyyyyy Godddddddddddd!!!!!!! !!!!!!"

BT went to the window and flipped his way on to the roof. He held on—barely—to the radio antenna. Sometimes he became a flag from the force of the wind and was hanging on with just his claws. The cats in the back had their little heads just a little over the side. When they saw BT flying, they ducked back down.

The doves were still trailing the van and Fred was tailing the doves. They neared the split. The van was still on the right. The light was changing from green to yellow. The van speeded up and so did Fred. Now the light was going yellow to red. The van was at the split and suddenly sharply cut from the right and crossed all the way to the left to go on Broadway. Fred couldn't make the same move and was still headed to Seventh Avenue. But just before the truck did, BT leaped from the truck to an SUV that did go on Broadway. The cats in the back of the truck waved as he landed on the SUV. The doves cut over to Broadway too. The van was only three cars ahead. BT, the athlete, was going to try some new moves. From the roof of the SUV he jumped onto the SUV's hood. The woman driving screamed. She swore she would never drink and drive again.

BT leaped from the hood to the trunk of the car in front of him. Now he was only two cars behind. He repeated this trick twice more. The doves covered their eyes each time. He was on the roof of a Ford that was just behind the van. The van had a little glass window at the back door. Cathy was there. She could see BT. BT yelled, "I'm coming for you! No matter where, no matter how far, I will find you."

He braced to leap onto the top of the van.

"One, two, three . . . " He jumped but just as he did the SUV turned down 45th Street. BT wasn't flying on to the top of the van; he was flying into the stop sign on the corner of 45th and Broadway.

Splat!

BT slid off the sign and down the pole to the sidewalk. He was stunned, not sure where he was. He had never been out of Greenwich Village before.

The doves sang in his ears, "Wake up!"

BT's eyes were spinning circles in his head. The doves tried to lift him but couldn't. Maya said to him, "Stay here. Don't move from here." The doves went to find Fred and the cat gang. BT saw cars and people going by in slow motion. He stumbled to his paws and began to walk down 45th Street, wobbling as he did. He imagined he saw Cathy in the distance. He started to run after her. He kept seeing her turning corners. He would run to each corner but he could never catch up. His banged up brain didn't realize that she wasn't real and he kept on and on until he finally collapsed, unconscious in a vacant lot on 15th St. and Tenth Ave. He had run for three miles.

The Bird Convention

• • • • • • • • • • • • • • • • • • •

The doves found Fred and the gang walking on Seventh Ave. and 55th St.

Virginia asked him, "Where's the truck?"

"Well, two police cars saw us go through the red light and were after us. We pulled over, jumped out and blended into the crowd."

"So no more truck."

"Correct, but we crashed it pretty good so it really wasn't worth saving. What happened to BT?"

"He didn't quite make his last jump and smacked into a stop sign. He's really banged up. We told him to stay where he is."

The doves and the cats arrived where BT should have been but wasn't.

"Yikes," said Sherlock, "he could be anywhere. How are we gonna find him?"

Old Eric said, "Not to worry." Then he walked up to the songbirds.

"Little ones, do you have friends"

The trio replied, "Are you serious?" Then they began to sing.

Another dove appeared and sat on top of the stop sign, then another, then three, then six, more and more, doves, sparrows, crows, starlings, all kinds of birds. They perched on signs, wires, window sills, building ledges, parked cars—hundreds and hundreds of them until 45th Street was Birdland. People looked up at the wall-to-wall bird convention.

One person said, "What's going on here?"

Another answered, "Maybe they're going to see *March of the Penguins*."

I dunno, but wasn't there a movie that started like this?"

"Exactly, I say we get outta here."

Maya, Virginia, and Stormy gave their many friends a description of BT. A blanket of birds flew off in every possible direction.

A Really Bad Ten Days

• •

BT was lying flat on his face, eyes closed. He heard some paw steps, but not cats; these steps were too heavy. Dogs! BT opened one eye. There stood Bowser and four of his fellow poochies. BT was thinking maybe he shouldn't have teased them all those times. "Well, if it isn't BT," Bowser said "—all by himself. You're not looking too good. Did you get hit by a car or something?"

BT was thinking how this was a really bad day. He didn't answer.

"What's the matter, cat got your tongue—no wise guy jokes today? I guess not."

The five poochies moved closer to the helpless BT who finally spoke.

"I thought the cats and dogs were in a truce."

"Yeah, with Fred, but he's not around is he?"

The mean poochies opened their big mouths and showed lots of teeth; they began growling. BT figured his day had come. Bowser enjoyed seeing BT's defeated face.

But then he saw BT get this big smile.

A deep voice said, "Is there a problem here?"

The poochies heads jerked around.

Big Freddie and the cat gang were behind the dogs. Fred was standing upright on his back legs, his front paws stretched forward. He snapped those paws and 12 switchblade claws flashed, 2 inches each, and so sharp they sparkled.

Bowser had an immediate attitude adjustment.

"No, no problem at all Fred. We were just gonna help your pal here."

BT recovered his boldness with Fred there. "Yeah, right, you were gonna help yourselves to lunch."

Fred told Bowser and the poochies, "Take a hike!"

They did, with tails between their legs.

Fred said to his best friend, "You look terrible."

"I feel worse."

Fred picked up BT and put him on his back. "Hold on to my neck, but don't choke me." And the gang headed back to Greenwich Village.

Old Eric spoke. "We shouldn't go back to bagel alley right away; there's too much heat there now; the petneppers might come back."

Fred didn't care. "If they do, I'll scratch their eyes out."

"I don't blame you, but we cannot take on humans. They have too many gadgets that we are no match for." Fred knew Eric was right. They would need to avoid bagel alley at least for a while.

That afternoon, Sarah returned home from the insurance company. The kids didn't greet her at the front door. Then she found the back door wide open and no Cathy and Heath-cliff anywhere. After an hour walking up and down Bleecker Street, looking in bagel alley, and asking neighbors if they had seen anything, she gave up. Her broken heart suffered a second time. After a week, she gave up looking. There was nothing left to stay here for so Sarah decided to return to England.

Also that afternoon, Lonnie called the advertising agency. "We've got just the exact cat you wanted."

The cat gang hid in an abandoned truck by the docks for about ten days. The doves were their scouts. Virginia said the coast was clear on Bleecker Street so they returned to bagel alley.

BT saw the *For Sale* sign in front of Purring Heights. The doves told him Sarah was gone. BT walked back to Bagel Alley, found his cardboard box, crawled in, and didn't come out. He was beyond bummed. He wouldn't even come out to eat. Fred and BT's brother Dandy brought him food and made him have some. There was no joy in bagel alley.

Part Two:

One Month Later
•••••••••••••••

At 8 P.M., the cat gang was in front of The Happy Cat Boutique; that is, all but Huxley.

The other cats were sitting on the cars parked in front of the store window waiting for the movie *Thomasina*. Huxley was still depressed and in no mood for movies no matter how hard the gang tried to get him to take an interest in something—*anything*.

Before the movie started there were coming attractions. A cat food commercial started. All at once, in a split second, nine cat faces smeared themselves against the store window. Cathy was in the commercial. There she was jumping up and down in love with *Gourmet Cat Treats*. Another girl cat was jumping up and down too.

Fred ran to BT's box. "Move, you lump, you have to see something."

"Go away!"

BT, don't mess with me now. Get outta that box. You've been moping long enough."

"Go away!"

"Cathy's on TV."

Zoom!!!!!!!!!!!!

A tenth face smeared against the glass.

BT went from comatose to maniac.

The cat with the creative imagination began to scheme.

The Pet Stars
• • • • • • • • • • • •

Lonnie and Leo had their office and kennel in an old warehouse in Queens, New York. A big sign in front said *Pet Stars, Incorporated.* Inside there were cages and a big set up for training the dogs and cats with ramps and hoops and all kinds of things for the animals to mess around with. During training, the animals would get treats from Leo for behaving. All the animals behaved because Lonnie and Leo were not very nice if the animals didn't cooperate.

They'd yell, "Do it right you dumb dog!" or "What a stupid cat!" Then the brothers would not feed the slow learners until they became better learners. The animals had no choice but to cooperate.

Cathy was in a cage, one that was bigger than the other cages in the warehouse. This was because she was a big money earner for Lonnie and Leo. She shared the cage with another girl cat, Phoebe, who was the other cat in the Cat food commercial. Phoebe was white with butterscotch tabby stripes that always reminded Cathy of BT.

Phoebe was a tough girl. She had been found on the street. Cathy had always lived with Sarah and John and knew nothing of the cold cruel world until she was kitnapped. When she first arrived at the Pet Stars warehouse, she cried for days and wouldn't learn to do the routines that Lonnie and Leo needed her to do in the TV commercial. She didn't get fed. Some of the other dogs and cats got mad at Cathy because she was getting Leo and Lonnie in a bad mood and then they acted even worse than usual.

Phoebe told Cathy to snap out of it for her own good and for the good of the other cats and dogs. Phoebe would hiss at any cats and dogs that tried to be mean to Cathy.

Phoebe began to teach Cathy the routines herself. Phoebe could be a very bossy little girl when she needed to be. Lonnie and Leo saw this and let Phoebe stay in the same cage with Cathy when they weren't rehearsing. Phoebe knew what she was doing. She wanted to be in the cat commercial too. The money makers were fed better and got to be outside of their cages more often, which meant the greater opportunities to try and escape.

Needless to say, Phoebe was cute too, like Cathy; otherwise Leo and Lonnie wouldn't have kitnapped her.

Phoebe had been a street cat in a gang that operated out of the Lincoln Center theater district in Manhattan near Columbus Circle. The theatergoers would buy lots of snacks before and after the shows. Phoebe and her gang would hang outside Lincoln Center looking adorable and people would gladly toss them some of their food.

That's how Lonnie and Leo first saw her. They had gone to a show at Lincoln Center. The next night L & L returned with shrimp and a net. Phoebe didn't get the shrimp but ended up in the net.

Now she and Cathy were good friends. They were going to be in a national Cat Show in two days and were preparing for it by learning special tricks to impress the cat judges. Cathy listened to Phoebe's stories about her gang and Cathy told Phoebe about BT and his gang, and then about how BT courted her and tricked his way into Purring Heights.

Phoebe said, "Your BT sounds like a very clever fellow."

"Oh yes, he is really smart. He will find a way to get me out of this. He promised me that no matter what he would find me."

Phoebe didn't think any one cat could rescue Cathy and she didn't want Cathy to live on false hope. "Cathy, don't hope for that too much, it wouldn't be easy."

"But Phoebe, you don't know BT; he can be very determined and resourceful." Little did she know how resourceful.

BT, Commander-in Chief of the Armed Forces

BT was in bagel alley, wearing an army helmet while standing in front of a blackboard and with a pointer in his right paw. The blackboard had floor plans on it. Fred was at BT's left sitting in the pink Jeep. The three doves were perched on top of the blackboard.

The fearless leader spoke:

"The cat show is today at noon. Our mission is to get in, free Cathy, and get out."

"We will divide into teams as planned." Then BT became a cheerleader.

"Strength team, are you ready?"

These were 20 dogs, led by Bowser.

The dogs yelled, "Yes, Sir!"

"Stealth Team, are you ready?!"

The cat gang yelled, "Yes, Sir!"

"Air Force, are you ready?!"

The three doves and one hundred of their bird friends, yelled, "Yes, Sir!"

Bowser, Maya, Tarzan, and BT had stopwatches.

BT commanded, "Synchronize watches!"

"Yes, sir!"

"Okay, let's roll!"

What a sight they were, coming out of bagel alley and marching down Bleecker Street. Their animal and human neighbors saw their determination and cheered. Then the crowd began to chant, led by Benny the bagel man.

"No more petnappers!"

"No more petnappers!"

Showtime
• • • • • • • • •

Lonnie and Leo were on the floor of the cat show. Leo was rubbing his hands and both had evil grins. Lonnie said, "If we win first prize, we get twenty thousand bucks and tons of free publicity. Then we can charge the ad agency more for having our cats in their commercials."

Cathy and Phoebe were in a small cage and not too happy. They looked around at the many other cages and the other cats didn't look happy either.

Phoebe saw all the unhappy cats and said to Cathy, "Have you ever seen such a miserable group. Only people enjoy cat shows. We ought to have people shows and see how they like being in cages and then having to do tricks."

The clock struck noon and the show officially opened. The public was crowding in and wandering up and down to see the cats in the cages. At 1 P.M. would be the opening ceremony. The crowd would take their seats and the cats would be let out of their cages to be marched around in circles while their owners held them on leashes for a cheering audience. Leo tied the leashes around his wrists in a tight knot so the cats couldn't get away. The march would be televised on the cat channel so it would have to start on time.

The songbirds had flown reconnaissance missions over and around the convention center the day before. At the back of the center were the big open bays where trucks would make deliveries. Today, a furniture truck was backed up to a bay. Two men were carrying in chairs and tables. Bowser's strength team was sneaking up under the truck. The doves were on top of the truck. Maya whistled each time the two workers carried in a chair or table. Then, one dog at a time would enter behind the men. This was repeated with the Stealth Team of cats. The 100 birds were flying overhead, waiting for their orders.

The cats and dogs were inside with Stormy. All were hiding in a corner blocked from sight by the chairs and tables that the deliverymen had finished bringing in. The little dove was to scout the convention floor and report back. She flew off.

BT has thought this plan out very carefully. The big TV in the Happy Cat Boutique had played the Cat show's schedule over and over. The cat march at 1 P.M. was the key to BT's scheme. Cathy would be out of her cage.

The synchronized watches were ticking down.

BT put on a headset two-way walkie-talkie and handed walkie-talkies to Bowser and Tarzan to put on too.

At 12:55 P.M. Stormy reported back to BT on Cathy's location. Then she went outside to inform the 100 birds.

12:57 P.M.

They birds came through the delivery bay and hovered over the cats and dogs. Maya, Bowser, and Tarzan were checking their watches.

Big Fred was sharpening his claws with a nail file.

The dogs lined up like track runners on their starting blocs.

The cats did the same in front of the dogs.

The birds became a formation like an arrowhead with Maya in lead as the point of the arrow.

The march of the show cats began to the opening notes of Beethoven's Fifth Symphony.

The stopwatches all beeped. It was 1:00 P.M. exactly.

The flying arrowhead entered the convention center and flew up to the ceiling.

Thousands of eyes on the convention floor and in the audience all looked up at once.

The stealth team of cats entered the convention floor slyly and sneakily gliding under and around tables, show displays, and people's legs; the heads of the people were still looking up at the flying arrowhead that was dashing back and forth. The audience thought that the bird formation was part of the show and cheered. The Stealth team's job was to get near Cathy, but stay in hiding, waiting for part two in BT's strategic plan. The cats found her with Phoebe. Leo was holding both on leashes as they marched with the other show cats. Leo and all the other people were still looking up at the bird formation that was swooping and sweeping like planes at an air show.

Emma eased into the cat march line next to Cathy, who was also looking up at the birds, as was Phoebe. She tapped Cathy with her paw. Cathy turned, was startled, but Emma motioned for silence.

Cathy knew BT had come for her.

Tarzan spoke into his walkie-talkie. "Target sighted! Put step two into action."

Bowser heard the command on his headset. He raised his right paw up. When he brought it down the dogs charged onto the convention floor. The dogs were barking and growling and knocking down anything in their way, including people. Chaos was everywhere, just as planned.

Leo held tight to the leashes on Cathy and Phoebe, jerking their little heads back.

Step Three.

Bowser and the dogs spotted Emma. They went right for Leo and knocked him down to the ground. Lonnie saw this action and tried to get to his brother, not to save Leo but to keep Cathy and Phoebe from getting away. The leashes snapped Cathy and Phoebe into backward somersaults.

Step Four.

Here come big Freddie and BT.

The two cats leaped onto Leo's chest and Fred stared that villain right in the eyes.

Leo's eyes were frightened big time.

Dead Ahead Fred stood upright on his rear legs, stretched his front legs out and snapped his switchblade claws open. Leo closed his eyes and thought he was history. Lonnie was almost there but Bowser and the dogs got in front of him and growled with their big canine fangs showing. Lonnie froze.

Big Fred took his big right paw and slashed the leashes in half with one great swipe. Cathy and Phoebe were free. Cathy and BT had a super nose nuzzle until BT said, "It's time to get out of here."

Phoebe thought she was going to lose her friend.

Cathy wouldn't let that happen. "BT wait, we can't leave Phoebe!"

But when Phoebe had been jerked back by Leo's leash, she sprained her leg; she couldn't walk, let alone run. Phoebe was ready to accept her bad luck, saying, "No, Cathy, leave me, go with BT." Cathy looked at BT with her big blue eyes. Fred stepped forward. "Don't worry Cathy, I'll carry her." Fred, the gentle giant picked Phoebe up and put her on his back where Phoebe put her front paws around his big neck.

Fred said, "Let's blow this place."

BT gave the command into his walkie-talkie. "All units, run back to the delivery bay."

Seconds later, the cats, dogs, and birds were running together out on Eight Avenue.

The last thing they saw was Lonnie and Leo running after them but the two brothers couldn't keep up with the animals. BT's army headed back to bagel alley.

Reunion:
•••••••••

That night was a happy party. Benny the bagel man put a radio in his back window and the gang was dancing the boogaloo. Old Eric wasn't a dancer anymore so he watched from the sideline. Benny also laid out bagels, anchovies, sardines, and Turkey Bites, and bottled water for everyone. Maya, Virginia, and Emma, emptied two water bottles into an abandoned hubcap and had a birdbath. Their wings splashed water everywhere. Cathy and BT danced and hugged all night. Fred didn't leave Phoebe's side and brought her all the goodies her little heart desired. Emma the matchmaker rubbed her paws together.

After midnight, the party was over and the gang settled into a snooze.

There was serious purring going on.

Old Eric rolled next to Fred. "Well, big guy, we had a good day, but I'm not sure if our troubles are over yet. The petnappers aren't going to let go of their big moneymaker that easy. I think BT and Cathy need to get out of town for a while and lay low."

Fred knew Eric was right.

The next morning, there were sad hugs and nose nuzzles all around.

Fred has a tear drop from his eye and it slid down a whisker. "I'm gonna miss you kids. Phoebe will be safe here. Her leg still needs to rest. The doves will go with you so we will know where you are. Do you have any ideas where you will go?"

BT thought: Sarah was gone. They couldn't stay in Manhattan. BT's brain was buzzing. He closed his eyes and waited for a vision to pop into his head and tell him what to do. He saw the living room in Purring Heights. He saw himself and John watching the Jets on TV. John had always told him that when he covered the Jets that Joe Broadway was a really nice guy. BT opened his eyes. "We're going to New Jersey."

Road Trip:
•••••••••

Bagel alley was just a few blocks from the PATH subway that went to New Jersey. The two went down the steps and there was a train map. The first stop after the train crossed under the Hudson River was Meadowlands Stadium where the Jets played. The train came and the kids got on board. The only other passenger was an elderly woman wearing a big overcoat. She saw the cats and smiled at them, leaving them alone. A minute later, the train pulled into the last Manhattan stop. As it pulled in BT and Cathy saw that many people were going to board the train. This was not good. The old woman saw their dilemma and softly whistled. As she did she opened the right half of her big overcoat. BT and Cathy jumped inside the coat and the woman closed it over them so they were out of sight.

The next stop was Meadowlands Stadium. The train arrived. The cats peaked out of the overcoat and when the other people got off, dashed out the door. The sweet old lady said "you kids be careful out there," and then she also got up and exited, but slowly.

The cats saw Meadowlands stadium and an overpass that crossed the highway below. There was a limousine waiting at the sidewalk.

BT wondered if it was going their way.

Cathy decided walking across was the better idea.

Inside the stadium the Jets were practicing for Sunday's game with their archrivals the Miami Dolphins. The Jets were having an uneven season with a record of three and three. The main reason was that quarterback Joe Broadway was playing up and down—one good game one bad game. Joe knew the team counted on him and felt the pressure. Miami was in first place. If the Jets were ever going to start a winning streak, Sunday would need to be the time.

Joe was standing next to his teammate and best friend, running back Curtis Martin who said, "I hear Mrs. Jameson is coming today and that she baked cookies."

Mrs. Jameson was the owner of the Jets. Actually her husband bought the team ten years before and she took over when he passed away. People said she should sell the team, but she couldn't do that. Her husband Jake had loved the team for 45 years, long before he was rich enough to buy the Jets. Margaret and Jake didn't start rich. Jake got into the steel business in the 1960s and made a fortune. Margaret and Jake didn't forget where they came from, which was just average working-class folks. They gave a lot of money away but Jake couldn't resist getting the Jets when he had the chance. Otherwise, Jake and Margaret didn't show off their money. Margaret still took the subway around Manhattan because she said it was a lot faster than it took the limo to get through traffic. The team had loved Jake and still loved Margaret. It was Jake who hired Jets coach Webb Milbank. The team loved Webb too.

Joe told Curtis, "She's a sweetie, but we need more than cookies."

Curtis answered, "We need for you to relax more and not take the whole team on your shoulders. Let us help you help us."

BT and Cathy climbed a fence into the stadium and nonchalantly walked onto the field like they belonged there. BT spotted Joe Broadway and the cats ran over to him and Curtis.

"What do we have here?" Curtis wondered, and he bent down and petted Cathy, and Joe did the same for BT.

Joe said, "They're pretty calm cats for not knowing us."

Curtis laughed, "Maybe they want autographs."

An assistant coach called for practice to start.

Joe told the cats he had to go to work and he and Curtis ran over to the rest of the team. The cats stayed on the field. The coach yelled, "Shoo."

Joe said, "Leave 'em alone. They'll know when to get out of the way. Besides, it's bad luck to chase cats and we don't need any more bad luck."

Curtis asked Joe, "Where did you hear that one?"

"I just made it up. They're cute; maybe we'll adopt them as team mascots."

"Can't hurt!"

When the players began practicing, BT and Cathy did know enough to go to the sideline where they sat on the players' bench and watched the action.

Behind them Cathy and BT heard a voice. It was Margaret Jameson.

"Well, if I had known you where coming here I would have given you a ride." She sat on the bench next to them.

During a break in the practice, Joe went into his gear and brought out a turkey sandwich. He took out the turkey and gave it to the cats and they snapped it up. BT told Cathy, "See, I told you he was a great guy."

Coach Webb Milbank came over to Mrs. Jameson and pointed to the cats. "I see that you brought friends today."

She said, "Oh yes, they rode on the PATH line with me."

Webb looked puzzled but said nothing. After all she was the boss.

When practice ended, the cats followed Mrs. Jameson, Joe and Curtis into the clubhouse. No one objected. The other players got a kick out of it, something to think about other than the big game on Sunday. In the clubhouse, the cats were treated to a water bowl and whatever food was around. Mrs. Jameson gave out her cookies and told the cats she would have cat food for them the next day. Meadowlands Stadium was their new home. The doves reported back to Bagel alley that BT and Cathy were safe and sound.

Sunday—And now playing for the New York Jets . . .
• •

The Jets were losing to Miami seven to nothing at the beginning of the first half. Joe had thrown an interception that was returned for a touchdown. BT and Cathy were watching the game on the sideline with Mrs. Jameson. BT was explaining the game to Cathy. She, like Sarah, was not much of a sports fan.

The Jets had the ball on offense. Joe dropped back to pass. He was being rushed and had to throw the ball too soon. BT winced. The ball was on an arc that would lead to another interception. Everything seemed to be in slow motion. The ball was coming down from the height of its arc. The Miami defender was setting in position; he began raising his arms to catch the pass and give Miami the ball back deep in Jets' territory.

The ball was just a few feet away from ending the Jets hopes of being in the playoffs.

A small caramel streak flew into the air and knocked the ball away and it wasn't intercepted. BT landed on his feet and ran for his life. The Jet fans went crazy. BT ran through the swarm of Miami players making moves unseen ever before on a football field while the Miami players fell all over the place empty handed.

Coach Webb was yelling, "Sign him up! Sign him up! That cat's playing next week."

Curtis said to Joe, "And I thought I had moves."

The Miami players and coaches wanted a penalty called for pass interference.

The referee shook his head. "No way! I'm not calling a penalty on a cat."

The Miami coach screamed, "But he interfered with the play; he prevented the interception. He should get at least an unsportsmanlike conduct."

The ref kept shaking his head. "It was an act of God, and I'm not penalizing God. It's just another incomplete pass."

The ref whistled for the game to continue.

Joe dropped back to pass again; he ducked one Miami player, then a second. BT was back on the bench holding his breath.

Joe threw the ball to Curtis who was speeding down the left sideline. Curtis stretched his fingertips, caught the ball and went into the end zone for a touchdown. The game was tied and their little mascot cat now inspired the Jets. The Jets won the game in a blowout and the game would go down in football history as "the cat game" and the throw that BT knocked down was called the "immaculate deflection."

After the game, everyone was back in the Jets' clubhouse. BT was a hero and Cathy was the hero's girlfriend.

Coach Webb sent the clubhouse boy out for tuna. "Get a case!!!!!"

Mrs. Jameson was petting her two new friends.

Joe said, "Hey, we never named these guys!"

And then Mrs. Jameson did. "As far as I am concerned, their names are King and Queen and they will be treated like royalty from now on."

The players cheered. Then Coach Webb stood in front of the new King and Queen but not for long. He got on one knee; the team did the same.

Webb said, "Fellas, hail to the King and Queen; they just turned our season around."

That night, the videotape of the football-playing cat was on every news show in America.

On Bleecker Street the gang saw their very own BT on the Happy Cat Boutique TV. They were overcome with pride. Big Freddie and Phoebe (now an item through Emma's efforts) were holding paws.

Dead Ahead Fred announced, "I think next Sunday we go see the Jets play."

Reunion:

•••••••••

When next Sunday came, the cat gang and the doves left early in the morning to beat the crowd. The cats would repeat BT and Cathy's trip on the PATH Line and the songbirds flew.

In the clubhouse at Meadowlands Stadium, the players were huddled around Coach Webb and Mrs. Jameson in front of a locker. In the locker, on two miniature thrones sat the King and Queen with little crowns on their heads and Jet jerseys. The players knelt again as they had done the week before. BT stood on his hind legs holding a sword. (Joe got it at Toys R' Us, which brought back memories of the pink Jeep.) BT held the sword, named Excalibur by Curtis, over the heads of the team. Coach Webb got up and began to clap his hands. The team got up and clapped too! Two assistant coaches came forward with pet pillow baskets that BT and Cathy climbed into. They all headed for the field.

The team came out of the runway. The fans cheered. Then the crowd saw the cats in the baskets and went insane. They began to chant, "King and Queen! King and Queen!"

The cats were placed on the team bench.

Some fans had signs: "Cat Heaven" and "King for MVC (Most Valuable Cat)."

The chanting continued, "King and Queen! King and Queen!"

The two teams went on the field waiting for the refs to start the game.

The fans now were chanting, "J-E-T-S Jets! J-E-T-S Jets!"

With all the stuff happening, at first no one noticed the line of cats scaling the fence. Then the cats started walking two by two behind the Jets bench. After what had happened the week before no one was chasing any cats away. The gang rushed to the King and Queen. Fred put his big arm around BT's shoulder; Phoebe kissed Cathy.

Fred said to BT, "So now you really are a King. . . . But don't get a swelled head."

Joe Broadway and his teammates made plenty of room for the gang on their bench.

Curtis said, "You know what they say, any friends of the King and Queen are friends of ours."

The fans saw these new cats and changed their chant to, "C-A-T-S Cats! C-A-T-S Cats!"

This cat insanity was unnerving the team on the other side of the field.

The Jets won in a blowout and more locker space was provided for the new members of their cat family.

Two months later:
• • • • • • • • • • • • • • • •

The big news in New York was that the Jets were in the playoffs. The team had won every game since the "cat game." The whole country knew about the cat squad that attended every Jet game, even road games.

Of course, people from outside the U.S. didn't always know about American football teams.

At JFK International Airport, British Airways flight 1118 landed on time at 10am on Wednesday. Sarah Fiore took a cab to Bleecker Street. Her real estate agent had told her there was a buyer for the townhouse. She had not been back since that terrible week and she wasn't thrilled to be here now. In England, she lived with her mum, and had begun teaching again. Still, every time she thought of John, she cried, and every time she saw a cat she cried some more.

She met the realtor at the town house. The sign she had made, *Purring Heights*, was still on the door. It hurt to see it so she took it down and put it next to the trashcan. She noticed the truck was gone. She assumed it had probably been towed away.

The realtor explained that the closing for the house was the next day. The buyer agreed that Sarah could stay in the townhouse after the closing and until she went back to England, which she realized was very, very generous. Manhattan hotels are just too expensive. She needed to stay in Manhattan for a week or two to tie up the loose ends of her life in America.

Also meeting Sarah at the townhouse was John's friend Martin from the Newspaper and Martin's partner Harold. John was to receive an award for his sports reporting and she would attend the ceremony to accept it. Martin and Harold wanted to help her in any way they could. The Jet playoff game was on Sunday, which was also Christmas Day. Martin and Harold told her that the Jets would have a Christmas Party the evening of the game in the Jets clubhouse at Meadowlands Stadium that they would be going to. The Jets owner, Margaret Jameson had known John and when Martin and Harold told her Sarah was in town alone, Mrs. Jameson asked that they bring her along.

Mrs. Jameson said she would send a limousine to pick the three of them up.

The following evening Martin and Harold picked Sarah up to go to the awards ceremony. They asked her how the closing went. Sarah told them that it was quick and smooth but that the buyer had a representative stand in for him as a proxy. She didn't even know the buyer's name as the townhouse was bought officially through the new owner's business. Sarah had been too distracted by her sadness to even ask for the buyer's real name.

After the awards ceremony, Martin and Harold escorted Sarah back to the townhouse. Sarah had been brave in accepting John's award for best football reporting.

At the front door Martin and Harold reminded Sarah about going to the Jet Christmas party on Sunday. She reluctantly agreed because they had been very supportive and helpful to her in getting through her New York visit. She really just wanted to go back to England. Still, there were a few more details that needed to be taken care of before she could return and forget about New York forever.

On Sunday, the Jets won the game so everyone was really looking forward to the team party later on. The cat gang had watched the game from the bench as always. At 6:30 P.M. the party began. At their lockers the cat gang was brought their own feast of tuna, chicken, shrimp, and, of course, Temptations Turkey Bites. The doves received gourmet bird food.

Mrs. Jameson had baked cookies.

The Jet players and their families were all present. The players' kids adored the cat gang. Joe and Curtis were not married but had fun with their teammates' children.

At 7:05, Martin, Harold, and Sarah arrived and walked into the clubhouse.

Sarah stared across the wide room at the back wall where the lockers were. Four eyes stared back. BT and Cathy charged across the clubhouse and Sarah dropped to her knees to embrace the two babies that she thought she'd never see again. The cat couple jumped into her arms and licked her face. BT (AKA Heathcliff) and Cathy were purring like freight trains. Everyone else circled around them. They didn't have a clue.

Mrs. Jameson said, "Well, my dear, it seems the three of you know each other."

Sarah told the story of the kitnapping, then asked, "But how did they end up here?"

Joe spoke, "They wandered onto the field and came right up to me and Curtis and have been here ever since."

Sarah stood up and walked over right in front of Joe, looking up into his face.

She remembered what John said the last night she saw him, which caused her to ask this question: "What position do you play?"

"I'm the quarterback."

Then Sarah fainted but Joe caught her before she fell. He sat her in a chair, Martin brought her water and Mrs. Jameson fanned her with a Jet pennant until she was conscious again.

Cathy and BT jumped in her lap.

The rest of the cat gang gathered around her.

Sarah remembered them, "Oh my goodness, these are the cats from Benny's Bagels!"

Joe said, "Excuse me."

"These cats lived across the street from my house. I don't understand any of this. How could they be here too?"

Joe scratched his head. "It's obvious that they all care about you and they should be with you—when the season's over anyway."

Joe hesitated then said to Sarah.

"And maybe then I could see you again. . . . I mean so I can visit the cats."

Sarah smiled. "Of course." Then she remembered that she had sold her house.

"But . . . but, I was going to return to England in a week. Now I can't; I can't lose my cats again."

Joe said, "Well, could I see you again and maybe we can figure out what to do?"

She said yes and went into her purse to write down her phone number and address. Sarah handed Joe the little piece of paper. It was his turn to faint. Curtis caught him before he went down and sat him in a chair next to Sarah. Curtis brought him water and Mrs. Jameson fanned him with the Jet pennant.

Harold thought, "What a pair?"

Sarah took Joe's hand. "What is it?"

He looked at the paper again and said, "This is your address—326 Bleecker Street and it's a townhouse."

"Yes, what about it?"

"I just bought it."

"Oh my God! I just sold it."

"Yeah . . . to me."

"No, not to you, it was sold to a company, a foundation or something." Then she remembered the name and understood; the name was the Touchdown Foundation.

She said, "It's your company."

"Yeah, although it's not a company; it's a charitable foundation."

"But why did you pick that house?"

"I was looking for a place in Manhattan where I could live with the cats when the season's over. When I saw the house, there was this adorable sign on the front door that said *Purring Heights*. And I thought that whoever lived there loved cats and that was the place I should get."

"I made that sign."

Once again she gazed deeply into Joe's eyes. She saw there everything she needed to know.

A year later: A Cat-happy Ever After

The pink neon sign of the Happy Cat Boutique is flashing on and off like a lighthouse calling home those who had once been lost.

At 326 Bleecker Street the sign is back on the front door of Purring Heights. On the second floor the fireplace is warming the big living room. Sarah and Joe are sitting on the sofa. Eleven cats and three songbirds surround them. Cathy sat on Sarah's lap and BT was on Joe's lap. Big Freddie was lying in front of the fireplace with Phoebe. Old Eric was next to them. All the cats were asleep and very, very happy.

Serious purring was going on!

Books Available from Gival Press
Fiction and Nonfiction

Boy, Lost & Found: Stories by Charles Casillo
ISBN 13: 978-1-92-8589-33-4, $20.00
Finalist for the 2007 ForeWord Magazine's Book Award for Gay/Lesbian Fiction
Runner up for the 2006 DIY Book Festival Award for Compilations/Anthologies
"...fascinating, often funny...a safari through the perils and joys of gay life."—Edward Field

A Change of Heart by David Garrett Izzo
ISBN 13: 978-1-928589-18-1, $20.00
A historical novel about Aldous Huxley and his circle
"astonishingly alive and accurate."
—Roger Lathbury, George Mason University

Dead Time / Tiempo muerto by Carlos Rubio
ISBN 13: 979-1-928589-17-4, $21.00
Winner of the 2003 Silver Award for Translation, ForeWord Magazine's Book of the Year ~ A bilingual (English/Spanish) novel that captures a tale of love and hate, passion and revenge.

Dreams and Other Ailments / Sueños y otros achaques
by Teresa Bevin
ISBN 13: 978-1-092-8589-13-6, $21.00
Winner of the 2001 Bronze Award for Translation, ForeWord Magazine's Book of the Year ~ A bilingual (English/Spanish) account of the Latino experience in the USA, filled with humor and hope.

The Gay Herman Melville Reader edited by Ken Schellenberg
ISBN 13: 978-1-928589-19-8, $16.00
A superb selection of Melville's homoerotic work, with short commentary

An Interdisciplinary Introduction to Women's Studies
edited by Brianne Friel & Robert L. Giron
    ISBN 13: 978-1-928589-29-7, $25.00
    Winner of the 2005 DIY Book Festival Award for
    Compilations/Anthologies
    A succinct collection of articles for the college student on a
    variety of topics.

The Last Day of Paradise by Kiki Denis
    ISBN 13: 978-1-928589-32-7, $20.00
    Winner of the 2005 Gival Press Novel Award / Honorary
    Mention at the 2007 Hollywood Book Festival — This
    debut novel "…is a slippery in-your-face accelerated rush
    of sex, hokum, and Greek family life."—Richard Peabody,
    editor of *Mondo Barbie*

Literatures of the African Diaspora by Yemi D. Ogunyemi
    ISBN 13: 978-1-928589-22-8, $20.00
    An important study of the influences in literatures of the
    world.

Lockjaw: Collected Appalachian Stories by Holly Farris
    ISBN 13: 978-1-928589-38-9, $20.00
    "*Lockjaw* sings with all the power of Appalachian
    storytelling—inventive language, unforgettable voices,
    narratives that take surprise hairpin turns—without
    ever romanticizing the region or leaning on stereotypes.
    Refreshing and passionate, these are stories of unexpected
    gestures, some brutal, some full of grace, and almost all acts
    of secret love. A strong and moving collection!"
—Ann Pancake, author of *Given Ground*

Maximus in Catland by David Garrett Izzo
    ISBN 13: 978-1-92-8589-34-1, $20.00
    "…*Maximus in Catland* has all the necessary ingredients for
    a successful fairy tale: good and evil, unrequited love and
    loving loyalty, heroism and ancient wisdom…."
—Jenny Ivor, author of *Rambles*

Middlebrow Annoyances: American Drama in the 21st Century
by Myles Weber
> ISBN 13: 978-1-928589-20-4, $20.00
> Current essays on the American theatre scene.

Secret Memories / Recuerdos secretos by Carlos Rubio
> ISBN 13: 978-1-928589-27-3, $21.00
> Finalist for the 2005 ForeWord Magazine's Book of the Year
> Award for Translations
> This bilingual (English/Spanish) novel adeptly pulls the
> reader into the world of the narrator who is vulnerable.

The Smoke Week: Sept. 11-21, 2001 by Ellis Avery
> ISBN 13: 978-1-928589-24-2, $15.00
> 2004 Writer's Notes Magazine Book Award—Notable for
> Culture / Winner of the Ohionana Library Walter Rumsey
> Marvin Award
> "Here is Witness. Here is Testimony." –Maxine Hong
> Kingston, author of *The Fifth Book of Peace*

The Spanish Teacher by Barbara de la Cuesta
> ISBN 13: 978-1-92858937-2, $20.00
> Winner of the 2006 Gival Press Novel Award
> "…De la Cuesta's novel maintains an accumulating power
> which holds onto a reader's attention not only through the
> forceful figure of Ordóñez, but by demonstrating acutely
> how ordinary lives are impacted by the underlying social
> and political landscape. Compelling reading."—Tom Tolnay,
> publisher, Birch Brook Press and author of *Selling America*
> and *This is the Forest Primeval*

Tina Springs into Summer / Tina se lanza al verano
by Teresa Bevin
> ISBN 13: 978-1-928589-28-0, $21.00
> 2006 Writer's Notes Magazine Book Award—Notable for
> Young Adult Literature
> A bilingual (English/Spanish) compelling story of a
> youngster from a multi-cultural urban setting and her
> urgency to fit in.

A Tomb on the Periphery by John Domini
  ISBN 13: 978-1-928589-40-2, $20.00
  This novel a mix of crime, ghost story and portrait of the
  protagonist continues Domini's tales in contemporary
  Southern Italy, in the manner of his last novel *Earthquake
  I.D.*

Twelve Rivers of the Body by Elizabeth Oness
  ISBN 13: 978-1-928589-44-0, $20.00
  Winner of the 2007 Gival Press Novel Award
  "*Twelve Rivers of the Body* lyrically evokes downtown
  Washington, DC in the 1980s, before the real estate
  boom, before gentrification, as the city limped from one
  crisis to another—crack addiction, AIDS, a crumbling
  infrastructure. This beautifully evoked novel traces Elena's
  imperfect struggle, like her adopted city's, to find wholeness
  and healing."—Kim Roberts, author of *The Kimnama*

For a list of titles published by Gival Press,
please visit: *www.givalpress.com*.

Books available via Ingram, the Internet, and other outlets.

Or Write:
  Gival Press, LLC
  PO Box 3812
  Arlington, VA 22203
  703.351.0079

3238510